THE FALCON BOW

Kungo's people, the Inuit Eskimos, are starving because the summer run of fish has failed them and the caribou herds have not yet returned. A hot-headed young Inuit hunter accuses the inland Eskimos of deliberately setting fires to prevent the caribou migration.

Kungo journeys inland with the magical Falcon Bow and discovers the truth. The inland Eskimos are also starving, and they are sure that it is the fault of the Inuit. It is up to Kungo to prevent a bloody tribal war—and ensure a lasting peace.

"Houston's prose takes readers to a world far removed from their own . . . where, with courage and a bit of ingenuity, great obstacles can be overcome."　　　　　—*School Library Journal*

THE FALCON BOW
AN ARCTIC LEGEND

WRITTEN AND ILLUSTRATED BY
JAMES HOUSTON

PUFFIN BOOKS

ᕐᑯᒃᓚᐃᒻ ᐅᓄᑦ ᖃᐸᑦ ᔔ ᐱᖓᕐᓈᓂ
ᓴᐅᒥᒃ
ᕐᔭᒃᓚᓄᑦ ᐃᓕᒃᓚᓄᔾ ᐱᔪᒃᓚᓄᔾ

To the Sikkusilarmiut of West Baffin,
your ancestors, yourselves, and your descendants.

Sikkusilarmiunnut Qikiqtaaluup Pingarnaani,
Saumingmi,
sivullisinnut, ilissinnullu, kingullisinnullu.

PUFFIN BOOKS
Published by the Penguin Group
Penguin Books USA Inc., 375 Hudson Street, New York, New York 10014, U.S.A.
Penguin Books Ltd, 27 Wrights Lane, London W8 5TZ, England
Penguin Books Australia Ltd, Ringwood, Victoria, Australia
Penguin Books Canada Ltd, 10 Alcorn Avenue, Toronto, Ontario, Canada M4V 3B2
Penguin Books (N.Z.) Ltd, 182–190 Wairau Road, Auckland 10, New Zealand

Penguin Books Ltd, Registered Offices: Harmondsworth, Middlesex, England

First published in the United States of America by Margaret K. McElderry Books,
an imprint of Macmillan Publishing Company, 1986
Published in Puffin Books, 1992
1   3   5   7   9   10   8   6   4   2
Copyright © James Houston, 1986
All rights reserved

LIBRARY OF CONGRESS CATALOGING-IN-PUBLICATION DATA
Houston, James A., 1921–
The falcon bow / by James Houston.   p.   cm.
Originally published: New York : M.K. McElderry Books, 1986.
Summary: Kungo, a young Inuit, seeks to prevent a bloody feud when
his people and a rival Indian tribe find themselves in competition
for dwindling food supplies.
ISBN 0-14-036078-6
1. Eskimos—Juvenile fiction.   2. Indians of North America—
Juvenile fiction. [1. Eskimos—Fiction.   2. Indians of North
America—Fiction.]   I. Title
PZ7.H819Fal 1992   [Fic]—dc20   92-4609

Printed in the United States of America
Set in Times Roman

CURR
PZ
7
.H819
Fal
1992

KUNGO JUMPED from the long sled and raced beside it, calling out to his team of wolf dogs, driving them across the snow-covered flatness of the sea ice toward the open water that lay between the mainland and the island of Tugjak. He was eager to reach the island and to see the old man, Ittok, and his wife, who had adopted him after the terrible death of his parents.

Kungo was short and stocky, with long black hair. He had the wide jaws and strong white teeth that come from chewing un-cooked meat. His face was tanned. His dark eyes, like those of all his nomad people, were drawn narrow from thousands of years of hunting across the open plain in the wind and glare of sun off snow.

Years ago, a band of Caribou Indians from the inland plains had killed Kungo's mother and father, through a tragic mistake, thinking them guilty of a crime against the Indians that they had not committed. Kungo had managed to escape, but he had seen his younger sister, Shulu, being taken away by the Indians. He had thought of her as dead for many years.

A surge of joy filled him now at the thought of Shulu. On the journey from which he was returning, he had found her alive, living by her own choice with the Indians. He had set out on his journey to avenge the death of his family, but when the moment came to kill, doubt had held him back. In seeking revenge was he any better than a mad dog, desiring only to bite and kill? In that moment of hesitation, when he was confronting the Indians, Shulu had recognized his voice and run to him. He might have killed her if he had acted in unthinking rage.

Now, to keep from being blinded by the bright snow glare of the early spring sun, Kungo pulled down the ivory snow goggles he had carved to fit his wide smooth cheekbones. The goggles had two narrow slits that let in only enough light to see by. Kungo was dressed from head to foot in white. His knee-high sealskin boots had been bleached white in the spring sun by Ittok's wife, and she had cut from the white underbellies of a dozen caribou skins his knee-length trousers, his parka, hood and mitts. All of them were white as snow.

Kungo reached back to feel the falcon bow, Kigavik, resting in its case with the quiver of arrows, to make certain it was still tied tightly to the sled. He was going to return it to the wise old man, Ittok, as he had promised. From Ittok he had learned the archer's art of handling the great bow.

"Harr, harr, harr," he called to the wolf dogs, his strong voice forcing its way out into the vast icy silence.

When darkness came, Kungo halted the team and fed the wolf dogs with frozen seal meat, then built himself a small igloo just big enough to crawl inside. To make it, he first licked both sides of his ivory snow knife so it was icy smooth. Then plunging the blade down into the snow, he cut and removed long narrow blocks of wind-packed snow. Each time he pulled a block, he set it on the edge of the knee-deep hole that he was cutting. In a short time he had the blocks circled all around himself and had started the second ring, spiraling upward until the low dome arched above his head. He reached up and fitted the last wedge-shaped key block into place, then crawled out of the low entrance and packed more snow tightly between each block. When he was finished, the small igloo was strong enough to hold his weight when he lay on it. Kungo threw his food and sleeping skins inside and crawled in after them, then wedged the entrance block in place against the damp icy chill that came rolling in from the sea.

Kungo's first chore was to start a fire. He did this with his small bow drill, the upper end of which fitted into a bone socket held between his teeth, while the lower, iron-tipped end fitted into a small hole in a piece of driftwood, filled with fine-shaved tinder, that he held in his hand. Kungo whirled the bow drill back and forth with such speed that the tinder in the hole began to smolder. He carefully blew it into flames, then lit the seal-oil wick in his small stone lamp. It glowed inside the snow house, lighting up countless glistening snow crystals.

Knowing that his wolf dogs were lying outside and would warn him if a bear came near, Kungo ate some meat, folded the white bearskin into a bed, then stripped off his clothes and rolled himself in a soft warm caribou skin. He slept until dawn came and lit the inside of his snow house dome.

With his ivory snow knife, Kungo cut away the entrance block and looked outside. The ice fog had lifted and Kungo gave a shout of triumph, for there in the black waters of the open sea floated the long white ice bridge that led to the remote island of Tugjak. It was the sight that Kungo had longed most to see. The cold spring mists rose off the water and in the distance before him stood the rocky island, its cliffs rising sharply like a giant's head thrusting up through a collar of broken ice.

The ice bridge, which stretched from the mainland, curved and narrowed as it reached out to the rocky island. Kungo could see that the bridge was beginning to rot now that winter was ending, and it was dotted by many spongy openings and dangerous cracks that weakened it. The slowly melting bridge would surely disappear with the next surge of wind and tide. He must cross it today. The moon was full and the flood of the next tide would be great. When the bridge to the island was swept away, another would not form until six moons had passed.

Kungo trembled at the thought of trying to cross the bridge, and even his lead dog, Amahok, the most fearless of the team, seemed to draw back in fear as it stared out at the icy blackness of the freezing waters. Kungo walked forward, jabbing with the butt of his harpoon to test the ice, wondering if it would be strong enough to carry the ten wolf dogs, the long sled and himself. There was no boat here, no other way for him to reach the island. He must try the crossing now.

He unhitched the lashings of the sled and slid off the dead weight of the big seal he carried. With it he fed his dogs to give them strength. He ate what he could himself, hating to leave behind even part of this treasure of meat, but what else could he do?

He relashed the long sled, carefully binding the falcon bow, Kigavik, in its case beneath the soft protection of the white bear-skin covering. He worked his harpoon beneath the lashings so that he could easily draw it out and he placed his knife in the top of his knee-high sealskin boot.

"Ush. Ush," he called, and the wolf dogs leaped to their feet and dashed forward. Amahok, running fast, guided the others straight out onto the dangerous bridge. The wind was rising.

Kungo knelt alert on the sled, wishing in his excitement to run beside the team, but he knew he must save his strength. He watched the moon's full face turn pale and fade into the cold morning sky.

As Kungo guided the team along the bridge, he could see loose pieces of ice in the open water being blown toward the frail pathway to the island. Beneath the sled's runners, the snow was hard and glazed with ice, caused by melting days and freezing nights. The sled slid easily with a crackling sound. Kungo watched proudly as every wolf dog fanned out on its own line, running smoothly, ears back, head and tail down, pulling hard.

When the wolf dogs came to the center of the ice bridge, where it sagged and disappeared beneath the water, Kungo halted the team. At the water's edge, the dogs whined and howled and shivered with excitement, for they sensed, as did their driver, the icy danger that lay before them.

Kungo drew his harpoon from under the lashings of the sled and tried to calm the team with his soft voice. Then, feeling before him with the sharp bone ice chisel on the end of his harpoon, he started slowly out into the dark water. He walked with his legs wide apart to keep his balance and to spread his weight over the rotting ice. He could feel the strong pull of the tide as the freezing water flowed over his high boots. He inched forward on the smooth slippery ice, his harpoon plunging into many holes. Yet he could feel that the ice still had some strength.

Kungo stopped, half turned and called to his lead dog, Amahok. Without hesitating, it trotted into the water and the rest of the team followed. As the sled passed him, Kungo leaped onto it and pushed with one foot, urging the wolf dogs forward.

In horror, he watched a tide-driven piece of ice as big as a white bear bump violently against the bridge. It struck hard and the whole length of the delicate ice bridge shuddered under the blow. But the bridge held together and the iceberg lay stranded halfway across the sunken path. The wolf dogs were almost swimming now, their backs covered by the freezing waters, but they held their heads high. Each searched desperately for its own footing, each one fought for its life. Kungo clung on top of the half-floating sled as he urged them on.

Amahok reached the small iceberg and scrambled around it.

Seven of the wolf dogs followed him. In a panic, the last two dogs held back, then tried to get around the other side of the small berg. There they were struck by the full force of the wind and tide. The rest of the team continued to pull forward, dragging the last two dogs back, tangling them with their long lines.

The two dogs were pulled beneath the water. Kungo leaped off the sled and holding the lines, scrambled forward, almost losing his footing on the slippery ice as he pushed through the freezing water. With his knife, he slashed the two long lines that held the drowning wolf dogs. The main part of the team was free and swimming. Kungo lunged at the sled with the whole weight of his body and his forward thrust caused it to slip past the deadly jam of ice that had almost cost all of them their lives. The remaining dogs pulled hard through the icy water.

Soon Kungo could see their backs, their flanks and then their dripping wet bellies, as the dogs found footing and scrambled up the sloping end of the bridge that rose toward the island. Kungo and the sled were free now of the freezing waters. His harpoon once more struck solid ice beneath the snow. Ahead, Kungo saw that the sky, the ice, and even the island, were hidden in a passing squall of snow. Big flakes came whirling down and disappeared into the blackness of the sea around him.

He halted the team and the wolf dogs spread their legs wide and shook the freezing salt water from their thick white coats. One by one they lay down and licked the blood from the pads of their feet, where they had been cut by the sharp crystals of salt ice.

Kungo stood amidst his team and looked at each of them. They looked back at him with their pale wolf eyes. Two of them had been drowned, swept away forever by the icy tide. I shall never again know a team such as this, he thought.

To the sea spirits he called aloud, "Those two good strong ones, those wolf dogs that have gone beneath the sea, they will pull the image of the moon through the water for you. They will pull it forever."

Kungo thought of those two brave dogs; his eyelashes froze with tears. He lay down among his dogs and did as they did. He rolled in the new powder snow. He was soaking wet up to the waist and his arms were wet to the shoulders. The dry snow drew the water out of his fur clothing. He lay on his back, holding his feet in the air to let the sea water run out of his boots. He rubbed snow into the damp fur, then beat and scraped it out with his mitted hands and with his ivory knife.

Kungo was tired and longed for rest, but he rose to his feet and urged the team forward, running beside them. If they stopped now in the cutting wind, his clothes would stiffen into ice and he, like the dogs, would freeze to death. As he ran, he could feel warmth return to his body. The numbness was driven from his hands and legs and feet.

At last he dared to slow to a walk beside the moving sled. He gazed up at the island that hung like a dream before his eyes. Almost at the top of its high cliff, he could see the two mysterious *inukshuks*, stone men, standing far apart, each as tall as a real man. Someone in ancient times had gathered rocks and built these statues with great care, long before Ittok had come to live on Tugjak Island.

Crossing the barrier ice, Amahok, the lead wolf dog, was guided by Kungo's voice. The team raced toward a narrow opening that led upward through sheer stone cliffs to the mysterious caves and whalebone house that lay hidden near the island's peak. When they reached the cleft in the rock, Kungo halted his team and unharnessed them. They could make their own way to the top. He was home at last.

Wearily he unlashed the white bearskin from the sled and flung it over his shoulder. Then, taking the great bow, Kigavik, with its quiver of arrows, and his harpoon, he slowly started climbing upward.

He had not gone far when a shadowy form appeared before him, its huge shoulders hunched, its mighty arms outspread. It was the powerful dwarf who lived with the old man and woman.

"Telikjuak!" Kungo shouted with delight.

"Is that truly you, White Archer? Have you returned to us alive?" called the dwarf. "So many moons have passed we feared you dead." Telikjuak then dealt Kungo a tremendous blow on each shoulder to show his friendship.

"You'll break my bones!" cried Kungo happily, overjoyed at seeing his friend again. "Here is your white bearskin. Thank you for it—it kept me warm." Kungo flung it into the powerful arms of the dwarf.

Looking at each other, they laughed. Their eyes shone with the pleasure of being together once more. Kungo followed the dwarf up the long narrow path and at last reached the sun-warmed circle of tundra moss where the snow had partly disappeared. It was surrounded by reddish granite walls rising higher than a man could throw a stone. Beyond the circle were the entrances to many dark caves and passages, and at the opposite side of the circle, dug deep into the gravel, was Ittok's ancient house. The roof beams arching over it were made from the ribs of whales, and at the house entrance stood two enormous whale jaw bones. The sod-covered sealskin roof and low stone walls were still partly covered with late spring snow.

"Ittok! Ittok!" the dwarf shouted joyfully. "Kungo has returned! The snow goose has come back to us again."

The old woman, whose name was Luvi Luvi La—meaning *sandpiper*—burst out of the house, cupping her hands to shade her eyes from the glare of the spring sun, trying to catch a glimpse of Kungo who was almost invisible against the snow in the white clothing she had made for him.

"Is that you, Kungo? Is it really you?" she cried.

"Yes. I have come back to you," called Kungo.

Luvi Luvi La covered her face with her hands and wept until she heard her husband coming. Then she turned to help him.

When old Ittok, bent with age, came out of the house, he stood in the harsh sunlight, his long white hair shifting round his head in the light breeze. He looked down, for he could see nothing with his blind old eyes. He smiled, for he did not need to see or hear this white archer. He knew inside himself that Kungo had returned.

Kungo walked forward and gently placed the big bow in Ittok's hands. Looking at the old couple who had adopted him, he said, "I give you all my thanks. This falcon bow, Kigavik, drove each arrow straight and yet not one man died because of them. My anger against the Indians has gone forever. At last I have found my sister. Now let me stay with both of you," said Kungo. "Telikjuak and I will hunt to feed us all. Let me truly be a son to you."

After the wolf dogs had arrived and been fed, Kungo lay down in the warmth beneath the arching roof of great whalebones. The lamp glowed in the little house and he slept as peacefully as a child. When he awoke, he sat up once more in his place on the wide fur bed and slowly told the old man and his wife and the dwarf the story of his long adventure eastward into the dreaded Land of the Little Sticks.

"When I arrived where the Indians were encamped, I was so eager for revenge, I shouted at them, calling them Dog People and Women Killers. That enraged them. They came running across the frozen lake toward me, many warriors against one. But they could not see me clearly, for I was almost hidden against the snow, dressed in my white caribou skins. I was able to dodge their arrows.

"I could easily have killed them with arrows from the falcon bow, but somehow I could not bring myself to do it. As I hesitated, I heard a voice calling to me. Then from the Indian tents, a woman ran out—my sister, Shulu. She had grown up and was married to one of the Indians whom we have thought to be our mortal enemies. I could see that Shulu loved her young Indian husband, Natawa. She dressed like a Caribou woman and told me she wished only to remain with the Indians who had captured her and who had become her family.

"Because my sister and her husband urged me, I stayed and feasted with the Indians, slept in the very tents of those who had been my enemies. For the first time, we understood how wrong our hatred had been. Shulu's husband, Natawa, whom I might have killed, was a young man much like myself, and although we spoke different languages, we became like brothers. I felt safe with the Indians and finally parted from them and my sister, sharing her feeling of contentment, saying that I would one day visit them again."

The old woman whose name was Sandpiper sat quietly and listened to all that had happened to Kungo. She was thankful that he had returned to them. She dried his fur stockings and his boots on the rack above the long delicate flame of her seal-oil lamp and patched the tears in his white caribou clothing, using skillful stitches so fine they could scarcely be seen. When Kungo lay back and fell asleep once more, she gently covered him, remembering all the nights he had stayed with them before he went seeking revenge against the Indians.

She glanced again at her husband, Ittok. He sat nodding— silent, hearing all, yet seeming to see or hear nothing. His long white hair, his pale staring eyes, his hands so gently folded made him look like a figure carved from ancient walrus ivory. She believed her husband had a mind so strong that, if he wished, he could send his other self to wander out between the moon and stars.

On the following day, Kungo walked over the whole island, feeling at last that it had truly become his home. He watched Telikjuak's team of wide-chested huskies and his own team of wolf dogs as they lay apart, eyeing each other with respect. Kungo and Telikjuak climbed the highest peak. When they reached the two human images, *inukshuks* made of stones, a

shudder ran through Kungo's body. As he stared out over the ice, he could see his long sled tracks. The twin lines extended to the very edge of the ice around the island. There they stopped, for the entire ice bridge had been swept away, leaving only the immense, glistening sea that stretched beyond their sight. Kungo and the dwarf looked at each other but said not one word.

Each day the spring sun drew closer and warmed the northern world to summer. Most days, Kungo and Telikjuak climbed high and stared out over the sea around them, looking for the birds or sea creatures they must hunt. Kungo was the first, one day, to see a thin black splinter moving in a windswept area of choppy silver waves.

"What's that?" he asked Telikjuak, pointing to the tiny object.

"I believe that is a kayak very far away," the dwarf answered.

They waited until they both could see it clearly. It was a slim kayak with one man in its center, paddling it masterfully with a long, thin, double-bladed paddle.

"He has courage," said the dwarf. "No man has risked his life to paddle out here in a kayak since the old man first arrived. I wonder what he wants of us."

As the paddler drew near, Kungo said, "Let us go down and help him with the landing."

The man who stepped onto the kayak stones was unknown to them. He had a serious unsmiling face with deep-cut lines around his mouth that made both of them think of hunger. When they helped him onto the landing, he said, "I am Pudlat. I come from the hunting camp over on the mainland. Inukpuk and the others sent me. Have you any food?"

From his parka hood Kungo took some of the sea pigeon eggs he had collected from the nests on the high cliffs.

The man cracked them open with his knuckles and sucked them down raw. The dwarf handed him others which he ate as quickly as he could.

"Oh, those taste good," he said. "I've been paddling for two days and the night in between without a bite of food."

"That is strange," said Telikjuak. "Is this not your time for caribou?"

"Our people were starving when I left our camp," the kayakman answered.

"Why?" asked Kungo.

"We do not know exactly why," Pudlat replied. "We only know that the caribou have not come down to the coast as is their custom. They have not arrived from the Indian lands."

"What has stopped the caribou?" the dwarf asked him.

Pudlat frowned. "We believe that many have been burned to death," he answered, "or frightened inland by wind-whipped fires. We saw a wide glow across the night sky, and day after day gray smoke drifted to us from the inland."

"What caused that?" Kungo asked.

"It is the Caribou Indians," said Pudlat. "To seek revenge against us, they have set the little sticks on fire. By burning the dried tundra moss and trees, they have killed or driven the caribou herds away from us. Our people are starving. Our children cry from hunger in the tents at night."

"I know the Indians," Kungo said. "I cannot believe that Natawa and his people would burn the trees to drive the caribou from you."

"You must go there and see for yourself," said Pudlat. "We need your help. We have heard the story about you finding your sister living among those Caribou Indians. You are the only ones who have met peacefully with them and can speak with them."

"We will do what we can to help," Kungo said.

Together the three climbed the steep path and inside the whalebone house they shared steaming sea-duck broth. Pudlat told the old man and his wife the sad tale of the forest burning and the fleeing caribou and of the hunger in his camp.

Kungo thought for a moment, then said, "I will cross to the coast and travel inland. I will try to meet again with the *Nenant*, the True Men, and my sister, Shulu. I will try to find the reason for these troubles."

"Dwarf-man, you must go with him," Ittok said. "I warn you both, be very careful." The old man stared toward them blindly. "Tales of evil, fire and hunger such as we have heard from this man are often not as simple as they sound." He continued in his gruff old voice, "I wonder what the Indians will have to say."

"It is simple enough," said Pudlat. "Our people on the coast are starving because the Indians have driven off the caribou."

"You remember my husband's words," the old woman warned Kungo. "If you go inland seeking revenge with the falcon bow, you might kill innocent people. Then the Indians would again seek revenge against Inuit families living on the coast. Once it

23

begins, that kind of trouble destroys both humans and animals until everyone is hurt or killed."

"I forgot—we cannot go," said Kungo, "for if we did, who would stay here to help you two survive the coming winter?"

Telikjuak nodded in agreement.

"I will gladly stay and hunt for them until you return," said Pudlat.

"You, White Archer, and you, Telikjuak, go and help the coastal people," the old man said. "Go together and discover the right and wrong of what has truly happened on the inland."

Luvi Luvi La nodded in agreement. Turning to Kungo, she said, "Adopted son of ours, you are like our bones. Though you say no words, I can feel your soul crying out to me. I can feel your longing to follow the trail inland again. Go then, both of you, to the Indian lands where your sister dwells."

Telikjuak and Kungo went out and crossed the sheltered tundra. "Come into my cave," Telikjuak said.

Inside, when his eyes had grown accustomed to the light, Kungo could see the dwarf's bed covered with the huge white bearskin and many curious objects propped against the walls.

Kungo stepped close to examine each of them. An ivory mask with green stone eyes amazed him most of all.

"Don't bother now with those ancient things," said Telikjuak. "I have brought you here to show you these." He started sorting through a pile of long and short pieces of driftwood that he had found around the island. There was no wood growing on this treeless coastline and to collect it had taken him many years.

"I would rather look at your strange knives and bear-claw necklaces and masks than those bits of driftwood," Kungo said.

"You can't make a kayak out of masks and ancient narwhal tusks," Telikjuak told him, "but we could make you one from some of these." He held up his longest, straightest piece of wood. "I have my own, and Pudlat needs his for hunting. You must have one, too, so we can leave the island."

"I would give anything to have a kayak of my own." Kungo laughed. "When shall we begin to build it?"

"Now," said Telikjuak. "Together we shall select the wood and bend and tie the frame with the strongest sealskin thongs."

This they did on the sun-warmed tundra, forming a spinelike keel, bending the thin upturned ribs with their teeth, making a long slender kayak frame pointed at both ends.

Next day, the dwarf went out in his own kayak and Pudlat joined him in his. They returned with four seals.

Telikjuak said, "We will need eight new skins to cover this kayak we are making. The old woman is already scraping and preparing three for you. Only five more and we will have enough. And also, the seals will give us enough meat to leave food behind and have some to take when we go traveling."

In two more days, they had not eight but ten seals, and on the following morning, they helped the old woman hobble down the long path to where they had placed Kungo's new kayak frame which looked like the bony skeleton of a fish. The old woman soaked and spread the sealskins and carefully lockstitched each one together. Then, singing a sewer's song, she stitched them loosely around the frame. By nightfall she was done. The kayak looked awful. Kungo and Pudlat propped it upside down on two waist-high piles of stones.

"Don't you be disappointed," Telikjuak warned him. "Luvi Luvi La knows her work."

Kungo could scarcely sleep. How could he ever reach the mainland in such a worthless, loose-skinned kayak?

Next morning, Telikjuak could not keep up with Kungo, who went leaping down the path toward the sea. When he rounded the big rock, he stopped dead as he saw his kayak. The night air had dried it tight as a drumhead. Kungo shouted with joy. Carefully they turned it over and admired its long graceful shape. Kungo ran up to thank the old woman and prepare all the harpoons and clothing they would need to take with them.

"We leave tomorrow, if the weather's fine," Kungo told the old man.

"Oh, no, we don't!" Telikjuak laughed. "This boy may be a wonderful archer, but he is not yet a kayakman."

Pudlat and Ittok both agreed with that.

Next day, Kungo and the dwarf climbed down to the small sheltered cove on the southern face of the island and together they lifted the slim kayak from its stone rack and eased it gently into the water. Telikjuak showed Kungo how to wash the sand off each boot before stepping from the stones into the kayak, for sand would catch under the ribs and wear holes in the sealskin covering. He told Kungo how to sit with his legs stretched out flat before him and how to paddle smoothly and silently, rolling the narrow double-bladed paddle on the wooden cockpit frame, and how to hold the paddle high and race with short fast strokes. He explained where to place each piece of hunting gear so that it could easily be reached almost without moving his body. Harpoon, line, knife, killing spear, three-pronged bird spear—each had its special place on the slim foredeck of the kayak, and behind the cockpit rested a blown-up sealskin float and meat hooks.

Telikjuak was slow on the land because of his short bent legs, but once seated in a kayak, it was very different. Working his paddle with his powerful shoulders and muscular arms that were thicker than most men's legs, he could drive a kayak forward until his slim craft seemed to shoot through the water like a fast harpoon.

While sitting on land, the dwarf and Pudlat both taught Kungo how to cast a harpoon. He aimed in every direction until he could quickly strike the smallest mark lying on the gravel. Each day, Kungo ventured forth on the sea and would return bringing home to his adopted family dozens of plump sea ducks, though he saw few seals.

In the long light of summer, the old woman scraped and sewed sealskins they would need for clothing. On their small island, it was a time of plenty. All the dogs were well fed and the meat caches were full.

"I feel badly being here with all this food," said Pudlat, "for I believe that my people on the coast may still be starving."

Next morning, Telikjuak called out, "Kungo is now a kayak-man. We should leave today."

Kungo stared up at the clear windless morning sky.

"Get ready," said the dwarf. "We are going now!"

The old man could no longer climb down the long steep path to the sea, but he came and stood outside his whalebone house. "Wife of mine, bring me Kigavik with its case and quiver," he called.

When he had it in his hands, he said to Kungo, "Can you still draw this bow?"

"I will try," said Kungo, and he took the falcon bow. He bent his head in thought, waiting until he could feel the magic trembling in his arms. Slowly he raised the bow and easily drew it full back, bending its curved horn wings into the shape of a rising falcon. He released the bow and heard its sinews twang against the sharpness of the morning air. Quickly he handed the bow to Telikjuak.

Taking Kigavik in his hands, the dwarf set his legs wide apart and drew in his breath. His jaw muscles flexed as he raised the big bow and aimed it north. His great back muscles bulged against his parka and his powerful arms swelled until they split the sewing in his sleeves. Yet he could not move the sinew string. Trembling from the strain, he lowered the falcon bow and gave it back to Kungo.

"I cannot understand that," Pudlat said. "You have many times our strength and yet you cannot draw that bow."

"It takes thought, not muscle." Old Ittok smiled. "Go now, White Archer, and take Kigavik with you," the old man told Kungo. "If you find real cause to use the bow, perhaps then it will help you."

Ittok turned away and with his old wife helping him made his way stiffly down into the whalebone house. Kungo stared at the powerful bow. It rested in his hands like a swift-winged falcon ready to strike out at its prey.

Luvi Luvi La reappeared, walking slowly toward Kungo. She carried with her a round bundle sewn tight. It was the size of a small child.

"Use this as a soft pillow for your head. Inside you will find all of your white caribou-skin clothing. If you fear enemies when they come against you, fighting in anger, then you may wear this clothing to hide yourself from their spears and arrows. But remember, it is my wish that these white garments remain sewn inside this cover. I do not wish you to harm other men." She brushed her hands across his eyes. "Travel safely on your journey inland."

Saying that, she raised her parka and allowed Kungo to kiss her breast, which was the greatest sign of a mother's love.

The old woman and Pudlat helped carry extra clothes and food down the path. They carefully loaded the inside of Kungo's new kayak with skin bags full of eggs packed in soft eiderdown. Telikjuak stowed the heavier load of seal meat fore and aft beneath the decks of his kayak. Carefully they arranged their hunting gear, making sure that everything was tightly secured in its proper place.

The old woman pointed up at the wide, thin, fish-tailed clouds that were beginning to spread across the sky. "You must hurry," she said, "or that wind will come against you. I fear for both of you." She wept. "Perhaps I shall never see you again."

Kungo tried to speak, but he could find no words to answer her.

Using their long, double-bladed paddles, he and Telikjuak pushed off from the kayak stones and stroked steadily toward the mainland. When Kungo looked back, the old woman was standing as still as stone, watching them.

They paddled easily, staying near each other, until well past midday when Kungo started squirming, for his buttocks and legs had gone to sleep. Telikjuak drew near him and they placed their paddles across each other's kayak decks and tied them tight. With this new steadiness, they were both able to slip out of their cockpits and rest themselves on the strong sealskin decks. They cracked open and ate a dozen delicious raw birds' eggs.

With all the numbness gone, they slipped back inside their kayaks and paddled on. The island had grown small and there was only a flat silver line of sea before them, so far were they from the distant coast.

That night, the early autumn sky grew dark and countless stars appeared. They rested again and ate seal meat and drank fresh water from their bladder bags, then paddled on and on, rolling their double-bladed paddles in a steady rhythm. Sometimes Kungo felt that he was working in his sleep.

By evening of the second day, they had seen no seals. That night, clouds came and hid the stars. Once more, they tied their kayaks together and slept until they were awakened by a rising breeze and the slap of waves against the low sides of their boats.

Quickly they unlashed the paddles, ate meat and drank some

water. "I do not like the look of the sky behind us," Telikjuak said. "This wind will be against us."

They paddled hard until midday.

"What is that?" said Kungo. "It's too big to be a seal."

"Keep on paddling," said Telikjuak. "We don't want him anywhere near us."

The dark head in the water disappeared.

"Whatever it was, it's gone," said Kungo.

"Paddle harder," said the dwarf. "I don't like it here."

Suddenly, a huge brown head with enormous yellowed tusks loomed out of the water not a stone's throw away from their two kayaks.

"*Ivik*! Walrus!" said Telikjuak, a look of fright upon his face.

"What's wrong?" said Kungo.

"He is by himself. That is what's wrong," said Telikjuak. "Walrus always band together in a herd, with lots of young and females. Not that one. He is an old male that has been beaten, driven out by a younger, stronger male."

As if the old bull walrus understood Telikjuak's words, it blinked at them with bulging red eyes, then ducked beneath the water.

"Keep paddling hard," Telikjuak urged.

But before they could dip their paddles twice, the enormous head appeared again, this time very close, right between the two kayaks.

"Look at him," Telikjuak whispered. "See the battle scars torn in his head. One tusk is broken at the tip. He's been fighting hard and lost all his females. Now he's out here alone and starving, with the bottom too far down for him to dive for clams."

The walrus swam toward Kungo.

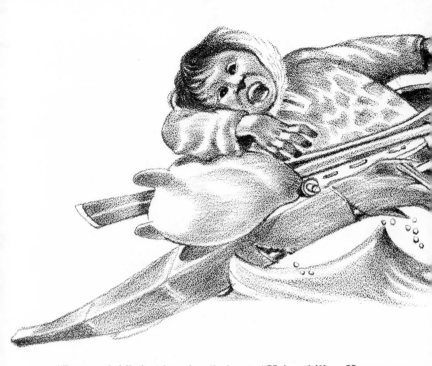

"Be careful," the dwarf called out. "He's a killer. Keep away from him."

At the sound of his voice, the big walrus turned on Telikjuak, eyeing him wildly. Then it raised its huge leathery bulk half out of the water and dove toward his kayak.

"Paddle! Paddle *hard*!" yelled the dwarf.

Kungo turned, slipped Kigavik from its case and strung an arrow. At that moment, he saw Telikjuak's kayak arch up in the center as the sea beast's mighty head and heavy tusks came surging up beneath the slender craft. The walrus roared. The old kayak frame broke in the middle; the sealskins split wide open. In a moment, Telikjuak's once sleek kayak was nothing but a twisted wreck.

Telikjuak struggled out of the broken cockpit and flung his arms around his sealskin float.

"Hold tight," yelled Kungo, knowing that neither of them could swim or survive in the icy waters. He aimed the arrow at the great beast's throat, but he could not draw the bow. The walrus dove. Then it rose again and went lunging at the broken wreckage, tearing the boat to pieces with its tusks, while Telikjuak clung to the float and kicked his feet.

Kungo tried again, but the big bow would not draw for him. The walrus saw Kungo moving and ducked beneath the water's surface. Kungo paddled hard to save his friend. Just as he was about to grab Telikjuak by the hand, the huge walrus's head appeared almost beside him. Because there was no time to take up his harpoon, Kungo lashed out with his long paddle blade and struck the beast across its bristled snout. The walrus gave a deep angry roar and plunged once more beneath the sea.

33

Now Kungo had the dwarf's hand in his. "Be very careful," Kungo warned him. "Crawl up on the back deck of my kayak. Gently. That's it, very gently!"

Perhaps no ordinary man could have done such a feat of strength, but Telikjuak did. Using his powerful arms, he slowly, cautiously eased himself out of the water and lay flat on the back of Kungo's kayak. Gasping for breath, his voice trembling from the cold, he said, "You'd better paddle away from here."

The bull walrus reappeared, once more attacking the wreckage of the dwarf's kayak, tearing the last sealskin covering to shreds, hungrily devouring the chunks of meat that it tore loose from the broken frame.

"Paddle as far away from that beast as your strength allows," Telikjuak told Kungo through his chattering teeth. "I've never been so cold in all my life. But this wind will dry my clothes, if I can stay alive that long."

The dwarf set his mind and his courage to survive and somehow he did.

At first light on the third day, they could see several rock islands. Beyond those the low coastline lay blue-gray on the horizon, rising into hills and distant snow-capped mountains. Far to the north there were immense icebergs with glittering blue ice caves parading slowly westward. Kungo paddled hard toward the nearest rock.

When he climbed out, Kungo said, "Oh, how good it is to feel solid land beneath my feet. Are you all right?"

Kungo had to help Telikjuak, who was so cramped he could not rise.

"Don't worry. I'll survive," Telikjuak said, as Kungo helped him crawl, then limp away from the water's edge.

34

They staggered up onto the island's rocks.

"What worries me," said Kungo, as they sat together eating eggs and staring at the mainland, "is that when we really needed help from the falcon bow, I could not draw it. Kigavik would not save you."

"No, you saved me!" said Telikjuak. "You didn't need that bow. Your quick blow with the paddle was what saved me. We didn't need to kill that beast; that is why you could not draw Kigavik."

The air was calm when they set dried seaweed afire and made a thick smoke smudge. It was easily seen by the people of Inukpuk's camp. They came out from the mainland in a large skin boat and rowed the two kayakmen back to their camp.

Huddled in the protection of a long low hill near the river's mouth, there were six skin tents. As well as the large skin women's boat, each family owned a kayak. Kungo could see them on their high stone racks safe above the teeth of hungry dogs. The person Kungo noticed most of all was Inukpuk's red-cheeked daughter who smiled at him, then turned her head when Kungo looked at her.

Kungo did not have to ask if these men and their families were still starving. He could see hunger in the bony gauntness of their faces when the dwarf divided their precious gift of island eggs.

"It is the Indians' fault that we are starving," shouted one young hunter.

"Almost no fish or seals have come to us this year," Inukpuk said, "and now we fear the caribou will never come again because the Indians have set fires to drive them inland. We have no meat cached. How will we stay alive this winter?"

The only food that had helped the sea hunters survive until

now was the sea ducks and the passing flights of geese.

When the next flight of geese flew over, Kungo went out with all others to watch them on their long journey south. The snow geese called down, "Kungo, Kungo, Kungo," as if they wished to give him some urgent message for the future. Kungo waved to the big white birds as they soared above him and he answered them, "Kungo, kungo," for he knew that they had given him his name and his helping spirit.

"We cannot stay here waiting for the snow to come," Telik-juak said. "There is too much hunger in this camp. We must go inland now and discover what has happened to the caribou."

"How can we do that?" Kungo asked him. "Walking day after day over the rough stony ground of the inland would surely tire your legs."

"That is true," said the dwarf. "I cannot walk that far, but these arms of mine should take me there."

"How?" asked Kungo.

"We still have your kayak," he said. "I could paddle it up that wide river. Inside it, I shall carry all I need. Later, when the snow comes, we will find some other way to travel. You have strong legs," he said to Kungo. "You can walk the riverbanks and if we come to violent water, we will both carry the kayak around it."

"Could you do such a thing?" asked Inukpuk. "It has never been done before. No kayakman of ours has ever had the strength to paddle upstream against the power of that river. When winter does come on the inland, and the river freezes, you will need dogs. Most of ours have starved—we can only spare you three or four."

"*Nakomik*, thank you," said Kungo. "That will be enough. If the weather is right, we shall leave tomorrow."

The first thing they pushed inside the bow of the kayak was Kungo's bundle of white caribou clothing that Luvi Luvi La had sewn inside a watertight skin cover. Then they stuffed in the dwarf's spare pants, boots and parka, as well as a white bearskin and two caribou sleeping skins, a small sealskin tent, Kungo's ivory snow knife, the meat-cutting knife, a small stone lamp and a square stone pot. Hunting and fishing gear, including Telikjuak's new fish spear and a three-pronged ivory bird spear, was lashed on the front deck of the narrow kayak. Kungo's extra clothing and gear was carried by the dogs in side packs.

"We are ready," Kungo told Inukpuk as he slipped the falcon bow case and arrow quiver across his back.

"You tie these over your sealskin boots," the wife of the seal hunter said, and she handed each of them a pair of thick walrus-hide slippers. "These will keep your thin-soled boots from being worn out by the rocks."

In their customary way of bidding visitors farewell, many of the young people walked along the bank with Kungo and the pack dogs. They did not follow far, for the hunger they suffered had made them weak.

The river was wide and deep and smooth near its mouth. For Telikjuak it was not too difficult to paddle upsteam, even though the whole center of the river flowed against the kayak. The dwarf wisely paddled near the bank where the currents swirled and eddied backward, driven by the central power of the river.

Only when Kungo and Telikjuak were exhausted did they stop and make camp near a small stream. Telikjuak put up their sealskin tent while Kungo rebuilt an old stone weir just below a series of small waterfalls. They had little to eat that night, but in the morning, Kungo brought in six red-sided trout from the weir.

Each of them stretched from his elbow to his fingertips and they had delicious belly fat.

The dwarf and Kungo both ate one whole fish and shared the rest with their dogs.

Each taking one end of the kayak, they carried it down the riverbank and put it in the water. It was shallower there with many small rapids. That made the paddling harder, but Telik-juak's powerful arms and great shoulder strength made it look easy to Kungo who, with the four dogs, kept pace with him along the riverbank.

Just beyond midday, Kungo saw a flight of black-necked geese with white cheek markings soar in low and land upon the tundra. He slipped the bow and quiver off his back and crawling forward, knelt and set an arrow to the bowstring. He tried to draw the bow, but Kigavik would not move. He tried again with all his strength, but he had no more luck. Finally, Kungo lay on his back, put both feet on the bow, and with both hands tried to draw the arrow. Kigavik would not bend at all for him. The geese rose and with a sound like laughter circled low above his head.

"I am going to throw this useless bow into the river," Kungo shouted in frustration.

"It is not yours to throw away," the dwarf called back to him.

Kungo was so angry with the bow that instead of returning it carefully to its case, he used it roughly as a staff to help him walk among the skull-shaped stones that were strewn along the riverbank.

That night, Telikjuak examined the bow and tried to draw it with his powerful arms. He had no more success than Kungo.

"This bow is good for nothing but a walking staff," said Kungo as he struck its end against the ground.

"If you keep on using it among the rocks," the dwarf warned Kungo, "the notch will break. Look how the bowstring is already frayed."

"I don't care," said Kungo. "This old bow is worthless. If I had bone and sinew, I would try to make a new one."

For six days they walked and paddled inland across the wide expanses of the Arctic plain until the mountains disappeared. Now the ponds near the fast-flowing river had white ice around their edges. Each day the sun rose late and moved crablike along the hills, disappearing earlier each night. When the stars came out, the whole world around them seemed to snap and crackle in the sharpness of the cold.

"I like winter best!" Telikjuak told Kungo. "Summer is the troubled time. Remember how awful it is to be bothered by mosquitoes? I hate those few hot summer days when all the meat turns bad."

Kungo laughed. "You're just saying that. I watched you out on the island. You didn't mind those gentle summer breezes."

At the end of the seventh day, they had still seen no sign of caribou. They shared the last of their food between themselves and the dogs. They slept and in the morning they approached the Land of Little Sticks.

"The weather is changing," said Telikjuak. "My twisted leg tells me it is going to snow. Each day the rapids make the water run too fast against me."

Telikjuak seemed tired and nervous as his eyes searched the low hills to the east. Small trees were reaching out onto the Arctic tundra.

That afternoon, snow began to fall. It was almost dark when they reached the first small tree. Telikjuak landed the kayak and hobbled up to the tree. He felt its twisted trunk and sharp needles

40

with his bare hands. It was dwarfed and gnarled, no taller than himself. The tree's trunk and twisted branches were permanently bent toward the south by the violence of the north wind that often raged across the open tundra.

"This is the first tree I have ever seen," he told Kungo. "When I was a small boy, we were warned to be afraid of trees and Indians, and I was told that they, too, were afraid of us."

"Twice wrong!" Kungo laughed when he heard Telikjuak say that. "Indians are True Men and the wood of trees will never harm you." He stood with the dwarf on a rock overlooking the country that lay before them.

Everything was hushed by the falling snow. Not a creature moved in the whole vastness of the land until suddenly a lone owl swept on silent wings over the windswept rocks, searching for any small sign of life, a lemming perhaps, to ease its hunger.

The new snow was so soft in this inland river valley that Kungo and Telikjuak found they could not cut blocks to make an igloo. The snow fell apart. Instead, they tramped out a hollow place in the soft snow and turned the long kayak up onto its side so it would help break the wind and erected their tent. Wrapping themselves in their robes, they lay on the white bearskin, truly hungry for the first time since they had left the coast.

That night the snow stopped falling and the full moon rose. It glowed like a ghostly human face, sending a long shimmering pathway straight toward them.

"We are entering caribou country," Kungo said. "The Indians must be near us now."

Next day, a lean black raven landed near their tent, hoping to find a scrap of meat. A killing wind moaned out of the north as ice grew out from the riverbanks.

"*Kaukpoonga*, I am starving," said Telikjuak. "These waters have grown too strong for me."

Upriver and as far as they could see, the waters were broken by rushing rapids that churned toward them, making it impossible to go further with the kayak. Far above the rapids, they could hear a distant rumbling sound.

"I am amazed that you could have paddled this far," said

Kungo. "Let us rest today. I believe we are coming near the singing falls. My sister told me she would return there with her husband. They may be camped there now."

Kungo crept out of the tent while the exhausted dwarf slept. When he returned, he had his skin bag filled with frozen chunks of mud. Rolling up some strips of dried tundra moss, he built a small fire and mixed the mud with water until it softened enough to stir smooth.

When it was heating in their pot, Telikjuak awoke.

"We must build a sled," Kungo told him. Using his knife, he split the sealskin cover off the kayak and the dwarf cut and sewed strips of it into harnesses for their four dogs. The rest they fed to the starving team while Kungo and Telikjuak gnawed and chewed on bits of it themselves. The strong juices tasted delicious.

They cut loose the lashings of the kayak's wooden frame and using the longest pieces, they bound them into two sled runners. Then carefully breaking the kayak's ribs, they used the pieces, tying them to form a dozen narrow cross ribs. Telikjuak cleverly curved the front of their new sled upwards with his little axe. Then rolling the sled over, they took the warm mud and packed it firmly along the bottom of each runner.

That night they made a thin soup by boiling the last scraps of kayak skin. The mud next day was frozen hard on both runners. Kungo smoothed it with his knife, then, filling his mouth with warmed water, he spat it along the runners which gave each a thick glaze of ice. Telikjuak turned over the long light sled, and when he gave it a slight push with his hand it shot smooth as an arrow across the snow. They had very little to load onto their strange sled.

As they started to travel again, the dwarf knelt on the sled and began calling to the dogs and pushing with his best leg. "Oh!" He smiled at Kungo. "I am so glad not to spend another day freezing my rear end on that cold river. It is good to be moving over snow."

They sledded eastward beside the open river and that night they could hear the waterfalls. Still the river did not freeze over.

In the morning, they harnessed their dogs and drove them up-river beyond a stretch of churning rapids.

That evening, as they were putting up their tent by the light of the rising moon, they heard a lone howl. It was answered by another, far away.

"Wolves," whispered Kungo. "Perhaps they sing of caribou."

"Treasure your hunger before a feast," the dwarf advised Kungo before they went to sleep.

Rising early next day, they hurried along beside the river rapids, desperate to find caribou.

Except for the lone track of a wolverine, they saw no sign of life as they continued on their journey for three more hard days and starving nights.

That morning, the dwarf eased back the flap on their small skin tent and pointed. "Caribou!" His voice trembled with excite-

ment. "See them. Over there!"

Across the river, Kungo saw first one, then two, three, six, ten. Carefully he counted on his fingers. There were seventeen of the brown-backed animals strung out along the opposite riverbank, moving slowly, heads down, feeding, using their hooves to scrape the tundra free of snow. The wide fast-flowing river lay like a black barrier between themselves and the animals.

"What will we do?" asked Kungo.

"We can do nothing." Telikjuak sighed. "It is my fault. If I had been strong enough to paddle this far, we would not have broken up the kayak. Then we could easily have crossed to hunt them."

"Do not blame yourself," said Kungo. "It is only sad that they are too distant for any arrow to reach them." Just looking at the plump grazing animals made his stomach churn with hunger.

"Those are the only caribou we've seen and they are on the move," said the dwarf. "They will be far from here before we find river ice that is strong enough for us to cross."

Kungo drew the great horn bow from its case beside the arrow quiver. "If only I could draw Kigavik," he said, then closed his

45

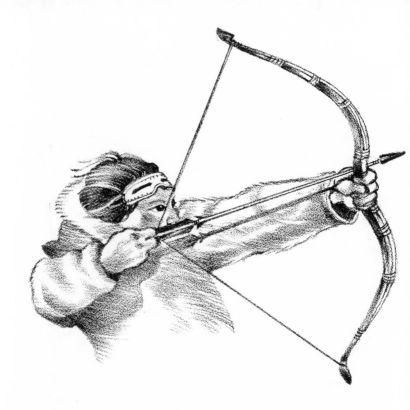

eyes and seemed to hear old Ittok whisper to him, "Use your mind, White Archer. Draw the bow!"

Taking the thick braided sinew in his fingers, Kungo pulled. The great bow drew back smoothly to its full curve.

"Quickly," said the dwarf. "Notch this arrow to the string."

Kungo raised Kigavik, aiming it across the river at the largest caribou. He released the arrow and watched it fly like a sliver of silver. The bull caribou staggered as it was struck through the heart. Kungo's second and third arrows put down two more of the wide-horned beasts.

Telikjuak handed him two more arrows and spread the powerful fingers on his left hand. "Five only," he said, "that will be enough for us."

The last caribou to fall frightened the herd. So excited was Kungo that he ignored the dwarf and notched a sixth arrow to the bow. As he was about to release it, the bowstring snapped. The caribou were running now, kicking up a haze of dry snow as they disappeared in the glare of the rising sun.

"The falcon bow has given us the gift of life," said Telikjuak. "Let us sled up this side of the river until we find some shallows or ice strong enough to cross."

They traveled eastward through a snowstorm all that day before they found a place at the head of some rapids that was shallow enough for them to cross the river. Kungo led the way. Cautiously their dogs followed, with the dwarf guiding the sled. When they reached the other side, they made camp and dried their pants and boots before they fell asleep, hungry and exhausted.

Next morning, they began the trek back along the south bank of the river. They were tired and staggering with hunger before Kungo saw caribou antlers jutting upwards out of the vast blanketing of snow. The dogs found new strength as they ran toward the exciting smell of meat.

They stopped beside the first caribou. The dwarf's hands trembled as he skinned and cut up the precious food and flung the first chunks to their starving dogs. Kungo hurriedly put up their tent. Then he and Telikjuak staggered inside with their mouths full of the delicious food. Wrapping their sleeping robes around them, they settled down to eat.

"Not too much at first," the dwarf warned Kungo, who was chewing like a starving fox. "Eat slowly . . . if you can."

47

When they had eased their hunger, Kungo looked out at the five large carcasses. "Will our slender sled carry so much meat?" he asked.

"Tomorrow we will see," Telikjuak answered. "There are no large stones here to build a cache to hold that meat."

In the morning the dwarf and Kungo ate again and with new strength they began to cut and pile the precious food onto their makeshift sled. When they lashed it tight, it left no space for Telikjuak.

"It doesn't matter," said the dwarf. "I'll lean against the load to ease my leg."

The four dogs strained against their harnesses as they dragged the heavy burden along the riverbank. Telikjuak cheerfully pushed along beside the groaning sled and Kungo pulled to help the dogs.

All the next day they traveled slowly eastward, seeing more and more trees. Before them, in the distance, a billowing ice fog rose like thick white smoke above the singing falls. Once when Kungo looked back, he saw Telikjuak's face twisted in pain. But they went on.

When it was time to halt the dogs, Kungo pointed to a tall empty meat cache that had been made by the Indians.

Telikjuak shaded his eyes. "I have never seen a cache like that one. It is made of wood, not stones."

"These True Men do not cover their meat with stones. They raise their food high in caches like this to keep foxes and wolves from robbing them," said Kungo. "Let us use this cache of theirs to pile our meat. Then you can rest on the sled."

The four-legged cache had a platform made from smaller trees bound together at the height of Kungo's head. He climbed the notched log that led up to the platform. Telikjuak untied the sled lashings and began flinging frozen haunches of caribou up to Kungo who caught them and arranged the meat. It would be safe here until they needed it.

Then Kungo helped the dwarf to feed the dogs and to pitch their tent. They ate from the one caribou they would keep with them for food.

At dawn, they continued upriver toward the rising mass of fog that glowed like silver in the morning sun. Kneeling on the sled and pushing with his strongest leg, the dwarf urged on the dogs for, like Kungo, he was glad to be traveling with his belly full of rich red meat.

"My sister told me that the waterfall that causes the fog is so powerful it keeps this part of the river open through almost all the winter."

"We may reach that waterfall before dark," said the dwarf.

Kungo ran beside the sled to encourage their dogs. But the dwarf was wrong. At midday, as they drew near the falls, the dampness in the air made the wet snow clog against their thin sled runners and they traveled very slowly. The full moon rose while they were approaching the falls. It spun webs of gold through the river's fog and turned the ice-laden trees and rocks into a magic place that seemed to belong in another world.

"I don't like it here," the dwarf called into Kungo's ear. "Too much noise. Too much moonlight. Everything is sheathed in ice. I would never sleep in such a dangerous place."

"Let's get away from here," said Kungo. He had heard of the frosted giants who, some said, lived in the dark ice caves behind the falling water.

Quickly they turned their sled and drove the dogs until they reached dry snow inland from the river. It was dark when they pitched their tent and ate and slept.

They had not gone far the next morning, before they saw a long line of snowshoe and toboggan tracks. They halted the dogs, looked carefully through the trees, then knelt to examine the tracks. They were soft and blurry in the snow.

"Indian hunters," Kungo whispered, "walking one behind the other. They passed here a few days ago." Kungo stood up. "We should follow them."

"Be careful," warned the dwarf. "These tracks may not belong to your sister's people."

Their team moved excitedly along the line of strange human tracks which curved inland toward the heaviest growth of trees they had yet seen. Beyond the trees were five thin columns of smoke feathering southward in the evening sky.

Kungo halted the sled. "Wait here," he whispered to Telikjuak. "I am going to see whose campfires they are."

The dwarf unlashed the soft bundle that was Kungo's. "Put on this clothing the old woman made for you, and be careful. I'll keep the dogs quiet. Make a signal if you need our help."

Kungo sliced open the bundle's stitching with his knife. Out billowed the snow-white caribou clothing. He took the little bag and rubbed white ash and seal fat on his face, then shivering with cold, he stripped off his sealskin pants, parka and even his boots, quickly replacing them with the pure white caribou clothing.

When Kungo pulled up his hood, the dwarf rubbed his eyes in astonishment. "With the snow behind you, you almost disappear from sight."

"I will go and see if they are Shulu's people," replied Kungo.

He started forward with Kigavik in its pale skin quiver slung across his back. Moving silently through the snow-laden grove of trees, Kungo wished that he had woven a new string for the falcon bow. Cautiously he circled south until he was downwind of the camp, for he feared dogs would scent him.

Carefully he parted the snow-laden branches and there before him stood an Indian camp with four small tents and one much larger than the rest, all deeply banked with snow. Kungo saw a few stretched skins hanging from the trees, but he saw no Indian dogs. Finally at twilight an old man whose face he did not recognize shuffled slowly from one tent to another. He was wearing a tattered caribou-skin shawl.

Kungo waited motionless in the numbing cold until the flap of another tent opened and two women came outside. They went to a nearby tree and started stripping off the bark. The younger woman began scraping the inner bark with a knife, collecting it carefully into the basket she carried.

Bending low in the evening's fading light, Kungo moved like the shadow of a wolf, creeping cautiously toward them. As he passed a tree, a thick powdering of snow fell from its branches. Nervously the older woman turned and looked behind her and would surely have seen him if it had not been for the snow-white caribou clothing that he wore.

When he was very close to them, Kungo squatted once more in the snow. Before the younger woman turned on her snowshoes, about to follow their trail back to the tent, Kungo recognized her thin face. She was the best friend of his sister, Shulu.

"Ramars!" Kungo called to her as he stood up.

The two women stopped in terror and stared among the long blue shadows of the trees. For the first time, they saw Kungo moving like a ghost toward them. Both women wailed in horror. Their snowshoes kicked the dry snow high as they bounded away from him toward the tents.

Kungo knew only a few Indian words and he called out, "*Nenant*, True Men! Greetings!" Then he quickly added the names of Natawa, the name of his sister's husband, Shulu, and his own name—Kungo.

Ramars and the other woman stopped near the tents and turning, peered once more in the direction of the phantom voice. Kungo pushed back his white caribou hood, revealing his black hair, then snatched off his mitts and held his brown hands open to them in a sign of peace.

Kungo heard Ramars say, "Kungo," to the other woman, then his sister's name, "Shulu," then many Indian words he did not understand.

Ramars pulled off her long mittens and let them dangle from their red-dyed cords as she, too, raised her hands to signal friendship.

Slowly, Kungo moved toward the two Indians. Ramars's face broke into a wide smile as she recognized Kungo whom they called the White Archer. They stood face to face, nodding their

heads in recognition, each speaking words in their own language that the other could not understand.

Ramars called out to the Indians inside the tents. At the entrance to the largest one, Natawa's father appeared. When the old chief recognized Kungo, he beckoned him inside. Breaking off a branch from a bush, Kungo quickly made a drawing in the snow showing one man, a sled and four dogs. Then he pointed back along his trail.

Natawa's father nodded, showing that he understood. Kungo turned and hurried away from them until he could signal to the dwarf who knelt on the sled and drove the dogs toward the camp.

Kungo jumped on the sled beside Telikjuak saying proudly, "You are about to meet the True Men, relatives of my sister's husband, Natawa."

Kungo had expected a fight to break out between Indian dogs and the four dogs harnessed in their team. But the inland dogs were gone, starved perhaps, or away hunting with their masters. Only older men and women and thin children came out and huddled together under caribou shawls, watching Kungo and the dwarf.

Kungo smiled at the Indians and said, "Natawa? Shulu?" Natawa's father only shook his head and held back the flap of the big tent and welcomed them inside.

The dwarf and Kungo blinked in the firelight of the long lodge as they greeted Natawa's mother and his younger brother and many others whom Kungo had known two years before. Kungo politely pointed toward the dwarf and said, "Telikjuak," several times. He was surprised that the Indians seemed to draw back in the shadows as though they greatly feared him.

When the greetings were over, they seated themselves around the fire and lapsed into silence. They had used up the few words they knew of each others' language. Kungo listened to the unfamiliar crackling of the wood fire.

The dwarf coughed and rubbed his eyes. "Too much wood smoke here for me," he said.

"You will soon grow used to that," said Kungo. "Oh how I wish we could speak to them," he added. Then he said again to Natawa's father, "Shulu . . . Natawa?"

The old chief and his wife nodded their heads when they heard those names. Natawa's father sent his younger son outside and he returned with a stiff roll of the yellowish tree bark that the True Men used to make their baskets and their swift canoes. While an old woman heated the bark, the young boy took from the fire some thin sticks that were charred black on their ends. When the bark was warm, the old man unrolled it carefully and laid it flat across his outstretched legs. Then, with the thin black twig, he made a quick drawing of a woman carrying a child, then a man with a pointed hat pulling a toboggan. The old chief pointed at the man figure and said, "Natawa," then at the woman and said, "Shulu."

Kungo smiled. "That must mean Shulu has a baby," he told Telikjuak. "I hope it's so."

Natawa's father outlined some caribou and pointed to the northeast.

"He must mean that Natawa and Shulu are away hunting. Have you noticed," said Kungo, "there are no young hunters and few wives here, and no dogs? Only older people and children, hungry children."

"Yes," the dwarf agreed, "all their faces are thin. These people are starving. No food here."

Kungo nodded. "Look, those two women are preparing to eat the skin of that tree."

The dwarf rose and Kungo followed him outside. They unlashed the caribou from the sled and many hands helped them drag it inside the tent. The older women cried out with relief. Soon they had the rich meat boiling in a big iron trade pot and every person in the camp was crowded into the long lodge with them, inhaling a mouth-watering smell.

55

When they had shared the food, the True Men thanked them. Kungo and Telikjuak lay down among the *Nenant* and wrapping their caribou robes around them slept in a circle with their feet toward the fire.

In the morning, Kungo again looked at the old man's drawing and once more pointed east, meaning Natawa and Shulu had gone in that direction. Kungo drew a sun on the bark meaning one day and Natawa's father held up eight fingers.

He paused, then drew a picture of two bears. One was on all fours, the other standing. The old man made a face to show that they were bad.

"He must mean that the bears here are dangerous," Kungo said to the dwarf. "You stay here and rest your legs and try to learn the ways and meanings of these True Men, Caribou Indians. I will follow Natawa's trail until I find them."

Kungo rested most of that day. But on the following morning hunger woke him and drove him outside. He threw the last of the caribou bones to the dogs. The dwarf and Natawa's younger brother helped him strengthen all the lashings on their makeshift sled and harness the dogs. Natawa's father came out and pointed through the trees along a faint line of snowshoe tracks that had almost disappeared.

Kungo nodded his farewell to all of them, then turned and urged the team through the deep snow, carefully guiding the dogs away from the trees that would entangle their long lines. Kungo followed the snowshoe trail until he left the shelter of the trees. Beyond them, the wind had covered up the tracks completely. He could do nothing but go forward, searching for any sign of Natawa and Shulu.

Next day, he crossed the river on the ice above the falls. Surely he would find them over there. From the top of a small hill on the other side, he searched the bleak white country that stretched endlessly before him. His heart leaped with joy. Far ahead was a long, thin blue track like a crack across the snow. He drove the dogs hard until he reached the new snowshoe trail. There he squatted, studying every detail. Yes, these were the tracks of travelers. Were there two, four or more? It was hard to tell, for they were hauling a toboggan and its smoothing surface flattened out the human tracks. Kungo judged by the lightness of the toboggan's print that it carried no meat. He tried to imagine Natawa leading, with his sister, Shulu, carrying the baby and perhaps helping pull the light toboggan. But was he right?

As he was putting up his tent that night, new snow began to fall. Kungo watched it come down, holding his mouth open to catch the big flakes. Icy blasts of air came howling from the distant Arctic coast, making the snowdrifts smoke as though lighted by some frozen fire. Sharp gusts of wind blew clouds of snow from every tree. The trees tossed and groaned like men whose feet are frozen to the ground.

Kungo took shelter in his tent. The storm grew and changed its direction, driving up along the river like a ghostly pack of wolves, howling as it gained strength and fury. It tore at the low entrance flap of Kungo's tent, pressing it in like some huge beast. Finally, when the little tent did not fall down, the storm went shuffling off along the almost-frozen river, searching for other hungry creatures.

Kungo rose in the first weak light of dawn and listened. The whole world was silent, blanketed by the heavy fall of snow.

He knelt, and with the full strength of his back forced open the tent entrance. He struggled out, blinking in the glare of the new white world around him. Long drifts of snow curved away like frozen white caterpillars as far as he could see. His four, thick-furred sled dogs lay almost buried, their bushy tails curled over their noses so that they could breathe. All signs of the trail he had been following were gone.

Kungo wandered aimlessly for almost a whole day. Then on top of a ridge he stopped and pushed back his snow goggles. In the bright glare, he saw a long new line of snowshoe tracks that disappeared into a narrow valley. He urged the hungry dogs forward.

They halted, sniffing wildly when they reached the tracks. Kungo knelt and examined the snowprints. They were the deep tracks of many Indians. The tracks were fresh, but were they made by True Men traveling with Shulu and her husband?

He started to follow this trail and his dogs pulled hard, whining with excitement. The blood-red winter sun had disappeared behind a low bank of purple clouds before he halted and pitched his tent. Kungo, like the dogs, had nothing to eat. He was so hungry that he, too, thought of eating the bark from the trees that stood silently around him. The stars came out and flashed their lonely signals to him from beyond the moon.

In the morning, he packed his tent and sleeping robes upon the sled, almost forgetting the falcon bow which he had stood upright in the snow.

He had not followed the new tracks far before he came upon a blackened ring of stones marked with spattered grease where the Indians had laid down tree boughs, pitched their tents, cooked meat, then slept around their fire. Kungo knelt and felt the ashes, then he licked the greasy stones. They were still warm and gave off a delicious taste of caribou.

Kungo stood up and looked far ahead, hoping that he would

see his sister and other True Men pulling a well-loaded sled. But instead he saw only gray icy gloom. The wind was down and the trees here seemed taller, thicker. Soft snow was piled high on every branch. He jumped when he heard the sharp cracks and groans that the trees made in the bitter cold. Off to the south he could faintly hear the steady rumbling of the falls. He looked at his dogs. They were alert, ears up, sensing that something strange was nearby.

A bit farther along, Kungo halted the team and made the dogs lie down in the snow. He went to the edge of a small stand of trees. Ahead, moving across a frozen lake on snowshoes, Kungo counted on his fingers *atouasik*, one, *muko*, two, *pingashoot*, three, now he was up to twelve, thirteen, fourteen Indians. Tall men, they were, and lean and hard. On their heads they wore hairy black bear masks whose ruffs hung down across their shoulders. They wore sharp necklaces of claws. The fringes of their caribou clothing swayed in rhythm with their gliding movements as they went forward in silence, the deep snow muffling every sound. These hunters pulled four long toboggans, each heavily loaded with meat. They had no women with them and were marching steadily in single file, their lead man's snowshoes beating down a narrow trail across the lake toward a grove of frosted trees. Each man carried several caribou spears and wore a large knife sheath at his waist. Some wore bow-and-arrow quivers marked with curious designs.

Kungo shuddered in the freezing cold when the last man paused and grunted to the others like a bear. These were not True Men, certainly not Natawa's people. Their clothing, their weapons, nothing looked the same. Don't move, he thought, remembering Natawa's father's warning against bears. He waited until these dangerous-looking strangers had disappeared.

He moved his dogs into a thick clump of trees, tramped down a space in the soft snow and pitched his tent, pushing snow high around it to give him warmth. He dared not light a fire, for in the clear, still moonlit air the rising plume of smoke would be seen from very far away.

After he had spread a white bearskin hair down on the snow, he went out and brought in all four dogs, placing them around himself for warmth. He spread his two caribou robes over them and in this way he survived the killing cold.

In the morning, he arose warm but as hungry as the dogs and traveled quietly away from the bear men's trail. The snow's crust turned icy as he approached the falls. There, the smooth mass of water rushed out from beneath the ice of the upper river and hurtled down over the rocks. The lower churning waters burst into a seething mass of white thunder, flinging up glistening rainbows of spray that widened into billowing clouds of winter fog, covering every rock and bending every tree with a shimmering coat of ice.

Fearing the thunder of the falls and the slick ice crust on the snow, Kungo started to move away with the dogs. They slipped and scrambled on the treacherous surface until the team split in wild confusion and entangled themselves around a tree. The gray bitch got excited and ran twice around the leg-thick trunk, then leaped over the big dog's line and crawled under the belly of the black dog.

Kungo could feel his skin boots slipping as he tried to untangle the team. Finally, he had to unharness the gray bitch. In the excitement, she ran away, slipping and sliding toward the edge of the falls.

"*Kiageet*! Come, you!" Kungo called as he went cautiously after her, using the big bow as a staff to steady himself.

When the gray bitch realized that she was about to plunge down into the tumbling rush of water, she turned in fear and scrambled back to the team. He harnessed her.

Across the roaring might of the river, Kungo's eyes caught a quick movement. He looked and saw the lean figure of a young Indian bent low, snowshoeing fast along the other riverbank. Kungo knew that it was someone he had seen before. His heart leaped with joy, for even in the icy gloom he could see that it was his sister's husband, Natawa.

Kungo cupped his hands around his mouth, intending to call out, but he could tell by the cautious way Natawa crouched and moved that he must be hunting. Caribou, perhaps, or had he, too, seen the bear men?

Kungo hurried along the riverbank. Beyond Natawa, among the ice-laden trees, he spotted the Indian meat cache where he and Telikjuak had stored the four caribou many days before. And, working his way slowly up the notched log ladder, was Telikjuak himself. Oh, I am glad Natawa and Telikjuak are hunting together, Kungo thought with pleasure. His sister, Shulu, must be near them, or safe with the other women back in the True Men's camp.

Kungo stopped when he realized that the dwarf would not be climbing into easy view if they had seen caribou, or if the bear men were near. Why then was Natawa hiding, as he moved toward the cache where the dwarf was now busy flinging heavy frozen haunches of caribou down onto the snow? The other strange thing was that Telikjuak now wore a True Man's hat of bark, with feathers fluttering from its pointed top.

Kungo watched in disbelief as Natawa made a sudden rush toward the meat cache, then crouched behind a tree to hide. When he saw the glint of Natawa's long knife, Kungo knew that something must be wrong.

Kungo waved his arms and shouted, forgetting that his white clothing made him almost invisible. Neither the dwarf nor

Natawa saw him in the clouds of river mist nor heard his voice above the roar of the falls.

Kungo ran back to the sled and drove the dogs up along the riverbank until he was above the falls. There he could see where thin ice had formed across the river. Would it be strong enough to hold him with the team?

The delicate prints of a fox's tracks showed where it had crossed. Taking long steps, Kungo cautiously followed the tracks, leading the team and using the falcon bow to feel ahead, testing the ice before each step.

When he was in the middle of the river, he heard a crack and felt the thin ice sag beneath him. A gray patch of wetness spread around him, soaking upward through the snow. Kungo dropped flat on his belly, spreading his arms and legs wide. Then, wriggling like a bug, he moved away from that dangerous place as quickly as he could.

The dogs ran around the soggy patch of ice. When Kungo felt solid ice beneath him, he rose trembling onto his hands and knees and crawled. Then, holding his breath, he leaped up and ran quick as a weasel to the other bank. The dogs bounded after him.

Kungo turned the team and drove them as fast as they would go down the opposite side of the thundering river until he was past the falls. Peering into the mists, he called Natawa's and Telikjuak's names, for he greatly feared what might be happening. When he drew near to the place, Kungo saw the powerful dwarf crouching up on the wooden cache, looking down at Natawa who stood below him on his snowshoes, his dagger raised to fight.

Telikjuak let out a sudden roar and flung a frozen haunch of caribou at Shulu's husband with such force that it would have broken Natawa's bones if he had not leaped aside.

They did not know each other. Even Kungo's sister, Shulu, had never seen the dwarf.

"Wait, friends!" Kungo yelled at them. "Telikjuak! Natawa! Stop fighting! I'm coming! Stop!"

But each fighter was so eager to outdo the other that they did not hear him. Kungo drove the dogs toward them fast, until they once more became entangled around a tree. Kungo jumped from the sled and ran stumbling toward the meat cache, with each step breaking through the heavy crust. In the softer snow of the clearing, he could see his two friends. He watched in horror as the powerful dwarf leaped down from the meat cache holding a frozen front leg attached to the sharp shoulder blade of a caribou. Natawa now stood tall above him on his snowshoes. Cautiously he circled the dwarf who crouched like a wounded animal, waiting for his chance to strike the long knife out of Natawa's hand.

Suddenly there was a wild shriek. Kungo turned his head and there was his sister, Shulu. She came bounding across the clearing, moving much faster on her snowshoes than Kungo, who was struggling toward the two men through the knee-deep snow.

"*Taima!* Stop!" Kungo shouted, as he realized that these two friends of his believed themselves to be desperate enemies.

Kungo's sister turned her head to look for her brother. As she did, she tripped and fell, almost disappearing in the snow.

Using all his strength, Kungo forced his way toward Natawa, who was now closing in to strike at the dwarf. "Stop! Stop!" He yelled and waved his arms, but so intent were the two fighters that they still did not see or hear him.

Natawa was circling boldly, tramping the snow down flat as he watched for his chance to lunge at the strange dwarf spirit that wore a True Man's hat. Without warning, he bounded forward on his snowshoes and, bending, lashed out with his knife at the dwarf who was crouching in the deep snow waiting. Telikjuak dodged the blow. Then with his mighty arms he swung the frozen shoulder blade upward, striking the knife from Natawa's hand. Its blade flashed as it spun in the air and was lost in the deep snow.

Natawa bent down just in time to save himself from the dwarf's powerful second blow. Then, snatching off one of his snowshoes, he used its hard edge like a sword as he hopped forward and swung at the head of his enemy. Telikjuak's bark hat tilted sideways as the hard blow sent him stumbling through the snow.

Shulu was on her feet again, running, screaming at the two fighters. Kungo was near enough now so that she recognized him.

"*Tuavi, tuavi*, hurry, hurry!" she yelled to him in their own language. "Natawa is fighting some kind of evil spirit. It is trying to kill my husband," she screamed.

The dwarf rose cautiously, guarding his head with his left hand, while with his powerful right hand he gripped the frozen shoulder blade, waiting for the chance to strike.

Shulu was very close to them when Natawa leaped forward and swung hard. The edge of his snowshoe caught the dwarf on the side of his head. Telikjuak dropped his club and reeled back, groaning and curling both his hands around his head. As he tried to rise, Natawa leaped upon him.

This was the moment that the mighty dwarf had been waiting for. He reached up out of the snow and locked his thick arms around Natawa's chest. Shulu heard her husband scream with pain.

"Stop! Stop!" Kungo shouted, for he knew that the great coils

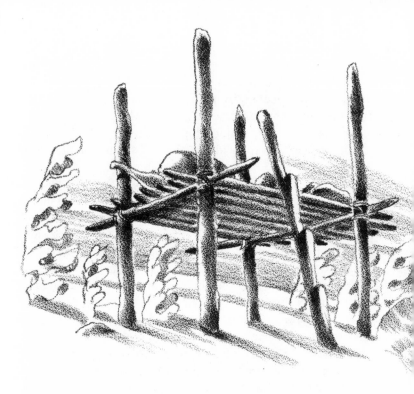

of muscle in the dwarf's arms and shoulders were so powerful
he could break the ribs of a full-grown polar bear.

"You, Telikjuak! Natawa, stop!" yelled Kungo, as he reached
his two friends and drove the great horn bow down behind them.

For the first time, the two struggling fighters turned their heads
and looked at Kungo and Shulu.

"Let him go! Let him go!" shrieked Shulu, as she knelt, trying
to force open Telikjuak's hands.

"Release him!" Kungo shouted, as he struck them both with
the falcon bow.

66

Slowly the mighty dwarf relaxed his grip on Natawa, allowing him to roll away in the deep snow. Both their faces were covered in sweat.

"Do you not know each other?" Kungo gasped as he held the horn bow between Shulu's husband and Telikjuak.

"Is he a man or a spirit?" Natawa struggled hard to gain his breath. He held his ribs. "If . . . I'd known . . . how strong . . . he was, I would never have gone near him," he groaned.

"Who is he?" said the dwarf, holding his throbbing head and glaring at Natawa.

"Did you bring this strange man with you from the island?" Shulu gasped.

"Yes," said Kungo. "He is the strong one I told you was my best friend. Natawa is lucky to be alive."

"So am I," said the dwarf. "That one," he nodded toward Natawa, "can hop on one foot faster than a raven and he strikes out very hard!"

"You two touch hands together," Kungo said. "You are both good men, good friends of mine and yet you nearly killed each other."

"That is true." The dwarf sighed. "I'm glad you came to stop us." He helped Natawa to stand. "Did I hurt your ribs?"

Natawa began to laugh, then winced with pain. "Tell him," he said to Shulu, "that it was my fault. I thought he was a bear man or a spirit. I tried to stop him from stealing meat from our cache."

"Tell your husband that Telikjuak wasn't stealing," Kungo told his sister. "Those are our four caribou—we piled them on this cache."

Shulu told Natawa that the dwarf had come out from his father's camp to bring back meat to the True Men who were truly starving.

"I am ashamed," said Natawa. "Starvation made me crazy. I was too quick to think you were an enemy. What if one of us had killed the other?"

Shulu's young husband groaned as he picked up the dwarf's hat.

"Your mother made that hat for me," the dwarf said proudly, as he replaced it on his head.

Working together, they loaded all the meat on the dwarf's borrowed toboggan. With tears in her eyes, Shulu turned and cried, "Kungo, is that truly you in those white caribou skins? Have you come back to me at last?" The three then helped pull the dwarf along Shulu's snowshoe trail. When they reached the grove of trees, Shulu proudly pointed to her baby, warm in his cradleboard where she had hung him safely in a tree. "There he is," Shulu told her brother. "Look carefully at this little one, for his name, too, is Kungo."

Natawa proudly took down the handsome cradleboard that he had carved and handed his son to Kungo.

"I can scarcely believe my eyes and ears," cried Kungo. "Imagine, I am now an uncle."

"What strange way is this to hold a child?" asked the dwarf. "Is that child so strong you have to bind him to a piece of wood?"

"No, he likes it there." Shulu laughed. "Babies resting on the board are very peaceful. That has always been the custom here among the True Men."

Kungo stared at the red-cheeked, dark-eyed child who looked solemnly back at him, then smiling, blew a bubble.

"Tell that strong man and your brother," said Natawa, "that we three shall always be best friends."

"Don't forget me or this baby!" Shulu cried with pleasure as she spread the fingers of her right hand. "You should say we five

69

are now the best of friends. Let's be glad that we are all alive—
together."

As they approached the True Men's tents, they saw that
everyone was out to welcome them and to thank the dwarf for
bringing in the caribou. Telikjuak followed Kungo into the large

winter lodge which was four skin tents laid together over one long ridge pole.

The older women prepared a great feast. Shulu lay back on the soft bed of boughs and skins and fed her baby. Soon he fell asleep and Natawa's smiling mother placed him in his cradleboard. As the meat boiled, the old chief spoke through Shulu.

She said, "These True Men wish to share and live in peace."

Shulu smiled at the dwarf as though they had always known each other. Natawa's aunt pushed the long log further into the fire and rolled it until it burned brightly beneath the big iron pot, sending shadows dancing across the tent walls. When everyone was gathered, Shulu reached into the steaming pot and speared five savory pieces of meat, first handing one to the old chief, then to Telikjuak, then to her husband, Natawa; the last two she saved for Kungo and herself. Then chewing a juicy bit of meat soft for her baby, she placed it in his mouth. Together they lay back in the long lodge with all the others. The steam from the boiling stew spread its delicious warmth until it almost hid their faces.

"We two came here," Kungo explained to his sister, "because we heard that your hunters had set the little sticks on fire to frighten the caribou herds and keep them from coming to our coast."

Shulu spoke Kungo's words to the True Men, who answered, "We did no such thing. We were fishing, all of us together, when that fire storm came in early summer. There was heavy thunder without rain. And jagged streaks of fire came down from the sky and split many trees. On that same night, we could see the tundra burning, and then the west winds came and spread the flames through the dry caribou moss. We were like the animals. We had to flee from the choking smoke. We know that many herds of caribou ran away or died in those fires."

"*Iounamut*," said Shulu. "There was no help for it—nothing anyone could do."

"The Inuit living on the coast," said Kungo, "believe that Indian hunters set those fires to drive the animals away."

"Never," said Natawa. "The caribou would not forgive us if we did an evil thing like that."

"We, too, were starving after the fire," said Shulu. "Only the birds kept us alive."

"We have never had so few fish come up the rivers to winter in our lakes," said the True Men. "We believed that some sly people dwelling on the coast had built strong stone fish weirs and set nets tight across the rivers, catching all the fish we needed to feed ourselves, allowing almost none to come to us."

"That is not true," said Kungo. "Our people have suffered, too, because so few fish came from the sea to run up the rivers."

"Then we have both been mistaken," said Natawa's father. "We have blamed each other because the animals and fish did not give themselves to us."

"Perhaps," said the dwarf, "the animals dislike the way we humans mistrust each other."

At dawn, a young Indian runner reached the camp, calling out, "Our starvation is over. The caribou have returned. Our meat caches are piled high. Our hunters are bringing in as much meat as their toboggans will hold."

The old chief clapped his hands. "Send others out to help them haul it here. Bring wood for fires," he called out. "Women, melt ice in the cooking pots and spread fresh sleeping boughs."

Kungo went out with the dogs to help the others, and they returned with the sled and their toboggans piled high with meat. Ramars and Shulu shrieked with joy when they saw their hunters returning.

Four days later, when the new moon first appeared, the chief declared a night of dancing and feasting to show the caribou spirits that the True Men were grateful for their gift of life to them. "Make sure that the drumskins are not broken, for we will hold a feast to mark the end of hunger."

"You will see," said Shulu, "there will be wonderful dancing in this lodge tonight. Everyone will wear their finest costumes. You, Kungo, will certainly be asked to dance."

Natawa's younger brother helped Natawa. Together they found stiff pieces of skin, then cut them to form a long caribou-like face with eye holes and outstanding ears. Natawa's own father snowshoed among the trees and cut two branches that were finger thick and spread like antlers. These Natawa's mother sewed onto the top of the mask, as well as cords to fasten it to his head. Natawa took black charcoal from the fire and darkened the mask around the eyes and nostrils, and rubbed red ocher in the ears and along the edges of the lips. The caribou mask was done.

Kungo and Shulu went into an unused tent and while none were watching made their own costumes for the dancing. They were no sooner finished than they heard the beating of the *Nenant* drum calling all of them into the long lodge. They all sat in widening circles from the fire.

When first they heard him, the children squealed with surprise. Natawa stepped from the shadows, his long fringes swaying. He was dressed as a caribou dancer. He held a hoof-shaped rattle in each hand. He began to prance like a young bull caribou, sniffing

73

the snow, searching, wheeling, turning as he began his dance.

At the far end of the long lodge, a second caribou dancer suddenly appeared, snorting angrily, pretending to paw the ground as it drew back for attack. Swiftly the combatants came together, circling the main fire. Then heads down, they attacked and locked their horns in combat. So clever was their dancing that all those in the lodge soon believed that they were watching two battling caribou. Suddenly the horned dancers drew apart and melted into the darkest shadows beyond the fire.

A heavy booming sound came from the entrance to the lodge. Many of the women screamed in surprise as they saw Telikjuak enter, carrying a huge Eskimo drum. The drum was flat, covered with caribou skin stretched tight around its narrow wooden circle. Behind him came Kungo dancing in the clever mask and fins of a huge red-bellied trout. Moving to the rhythm of Telikjuak's drum, Kungo seemed to swim down the whole length of the long lodge, twisting and turning like a fish, waving his fins as he opened and closed the lower jaw of his clever mask. There was a roar of pleasure from the Indians.

When Kungo's wonderful swimming dance was done, the drumming stopped and a wild pebble-tapping came from the hand rattles that the women held up near the fire. Shulu seemed to fly through the entrance to the lodge. Bent forward like a diving falcon, with white wings stretched behind her, she whirled, swift as a hawk rising into the air. Her eyes flashed in the firelight, as their dark pupils peered out through a short-beaked bird mask. Natawa shouted with pride and all the True Men slapped their knees in rhythm with the women's shaking rattles. Shulu's moccasins barely touched the ground. She leaped gracefully between the shadows in the flickering firelight. Dancing among

75

the guests, she raised her white wings high above their heads, the long fringes on her costume ruffling out like falcon feathers.

When the feasting had ended, Kungo lay back, enjoying the low flickering firelight and the pungent odor of fresh-cut spruce boughs. Here he was at last with his sister, her Indian husband and their wonderful new child in the middle of what he had once thought an enemy Indian camp. He had never felt more welcome anywhere in all his life. Here in the warmth of the long lodge, he felt as though he were a True Man. These very persons whom he had once—a long time ago—set out to kill had now turned into his dearest relatives and friends. How, he wondered, could he or more recently the dwarf have ever wished to harm them?

During the long bright days of spring, the air warmed and the winter snows in the forest melted and ran into the river in countless streams. The river rose and like a giant broke its winter bonds, flinging huge chunks of ice hurtling over the falls to smash on the boulders below. Small trees were uprooted and carried away in the rushing brown water. High above the flood-fed river, long wavering flights of snow geese appeared, sending their wild music down to the land. Kungo threw back his head and answered them, "Kungo, kungo, kungo." The return of these great birds marked the changing of the season.

"I like living here with True Men," Telikjuak told Kungo, "but when the river clears, we must return to the coast. Our people may still be starving."

As the last spring moon grew old, the dwarf and Kungo watched Natawa's uncle, Pashak, who squatted on the riverbank, carefully repairing his bark canoe. When it was finished, he put it in the river and showed them how to kneel gently in its bow and stern and paddle it with skill. At first the frail canoe seemed to tremble like a leaf. But because they were skillful kayakmen, they learned every lesson that Pashak taught them and soon could paddle silently and swiftly on the river.

"Tomorrow comes the new moon," the dwarf said, "a lucky day for us to begin our journey to the coast."

"Will you not come with us?" said Kungo to his sister and to Natawa.

"That is for my husband to decide," Shulu answered.

"Yes, we will gladly go with you," said Natawa. "Shulu and our son should see the land where she was born."

To each of the four Indian families who prepared a canoe to go with them, Kungo and Telikjuak gave one of their dogs, saying, "We hope their offspring will replace the dogs that you have lost."

The True Men answered, "Return and live with us in any season, enjoy our country."

Into the five canoes the travelers packed as much meat as they could safely hold. Kungo and the dwarf placed the falcon bow, their tent and all their hunting gear in their canoe. Natawa and Shulu with their child were in the first canoe that pushed off from the riverbank. Kungo climbed cautiously into the bow of the second bark canoe, while Telikjuak knelt in the stern. The third canoe had the heaviest load of meat and was paddled by Pashak and his brother. The last two canoes had strong paddlers, for they, too, were loaded with tents, sleeping skins and meat.

"Safe journeying," Natawa's father called to them from the riverbank.

The Caribou Indians stood still and watchful, trying to imagine the excitement of their countrymen when they reached the coast and first saw strange humans and walrus and white bears.

"Farewell to all of you," Kungo and the dwarf called back to the Indians as the canoes were caught and carried westward by the swift current of the river.

Kungo and Telikjuak enjoyed the lightness of their delicate bark canoe, but using short single-bladed paddles, they could not keep up with the True Men. When they rested at midday, Telikjuak told Shulu he was going to try his kayak paddle.

Natawa said, "It may look strange, but you must surely try it."

Stroking with his kayak paddle, the dwarf's great strength caused their canoe to pass all the others until they were beside Natawa in his lead canoe.

Shulu smiled at the dwarf. "You have found the best way to travel on this river."

Passing through Indian country, Kungo wondered at the new spring growth of tender green leaves and small star-shaped flowers. Sandpipers hopped along the water's edge, building their nests. Everywhere there was the rich smell of the trees as the winds set them whispering to all the creatures of the earth.

The light was fading when they stopped and pitched their tents, lit fires, then ate and slept.

Shulu rose early, fed her baby and tied him safely to his cradleboard. When her brother woke, the baby smiled and seemed to wink at him as though they shared some secret from the past. The Indians broke camp and paddled quickly through the burnt land.

On the fourth morning at the end of the tree country, they saw a black bear and her cub running unafraid along the riverbank, keeping pace with the five canoes. Their loose-fitting, blue-black coats rippled in the sunlight. The female bear looked back often to be sure her cub was following her.

Shulu called farewell to the *usqua* and her young one. The black bear seemed to understand, for she stopped and sat up like a human on the mossy riverbank and breastfed her hungry cub.

At the end of the fifth day of paddling, they followed the river far out on the barrens and could see a wide silver glow along the coast.

"I can't get used to it," said Natawa. "How could they live out here without the trees?"

"I've grown to be like you," Shulu whispered to her husband. "I, too, miss the trees. But don't tell my brother I said that."

Because of the high water, they passed safely over many rapids. On the ninth morning, after they had packed their canoes, Shulu hurried up a bare rock hill with Kungo.

"We can see it!" she called down to the others. "The sea is shining just ahead of us." She clutched her brother's arm and started weeping. "Mother, father," she sobbed, "I am so glad to be coming home."

"So am I," said Kungo, though they both knew they had no living mother or father and no real home to return to.

Before them the barren lands of rock and tundra sloped down toward the coast and the smooth-flowing river widened, turning blue-green as it mixed with the tidal waters of the sea.

"Look," said Kungo, trying to cheer his sister. "There at the river's mouth, that is where Inukpuk and the sea hunters make their camp."

That night the early summer sky did not grow dark and Telik-juak said, "If we leave early in the morning, we should reach their camp tomorrow."

They paddled hard next day and just at evening all five canoes drifted offshore before the scattering of Inuit tents. Not a single person appeared to greet them.

"What has happened? Can they all be dead?" asked Kungo.

"No," said Telikjuak, "see their dogs. If we two had returned alone in kayaks, they would all be out to welcome us. They are being cautious, seeing strangers in canoes."

With that, the dwarf picked up his double-bladed paddle and started stroking in the style of a kayakman, calling out, *"Tikiposi*, we have arrived! Friends! Cousins! We have returned!"

One by one, the men, women and children from the sea hunters' camp appeared.

"Is that you, Kungo, and the island man?" Inukpuk called to them in Inuktitut.

"Ayii," Kungo shouted, "yes. We have come back bringing friends."

When the hunters heard Kungo's words, they came cautiously down to the riverbank, looking thin and hungry.

"What strange boats are these?" Inukpuk called. "And who are those foreigners with you?"

"This one is no foreigner," Kungo told them. "She is my sister, Shulu, who has married a True Man and started a family while living with him in the uplands."

Inukpuk's wife said, "I have heard the story of your sister, but she is dressed like no woman I have ever seen. And who are those others?"

"These are True Men," shouted the dwarf. "Caribou hunters like ourselves. This is the first time they have ever seen the sea. They have filled their canoes with a gift of meat for you."

"Quickly, come ashore," called Inukpuk. "Many here are hungry."

"How can they be starving?" one of the Indians asked Shulu. "We thought they had kept all of the fish from us."

"They have no fish drying, as you can see," Shulu answered as she pointed at the camp, "and only a few dogs. Theirs, like ours, have died."

When they landed, the True Men gave away all the meat and set up their tents near the Inuit camp and joined in the feasting. Shulu spoke both their languages, so that for the first time these neighboring people came to understand each other.

Kungo heard one old woman whisper to another, "I was always told that Indians were bad, but I like them. That husband of Shulu's has such a handsome face. Their baby looks just like him."

A few days later, Inuit hunters spied herds of caribou in the hills behind their camp. "We were wrong," Inukpuk said, "the animals have come back to us."

For half a moon, the seven True Men remained beside the sea hunters' camp. They tried paddling kayaks and the sea hunters used their canoes. The seals returned in numbers. And when the fish arrived, they joined together and speared as many as they

needed. The True Men could see that the Inuit had not held back the fish from going up the river. And always Kungo, Shulu and the dwarf encouraged all of them to be friends together.

When they saw the fish swimming up the river, the canoe men said, "We must go with them, for we have a longing to see our families once again."

"Tell my father we shall stay by the sea for several moons," said Natawa, "but later we hope to return to him."

Next morning, all the Indian tents were gone and their four canoes had disappeared. Only Natawa and Shulu remained behind.

"We also must leave," said Kungo, "and try to reach the island of Tugjak. I am eager to show the old man and the old woman my sister and her husband, and to let them see that I have become an uncle!"

"You are welcome to borrow our umiak," Inukpuk said, "if later one of you will help Pudlat sail it back to us."

"We will do that," said the dwarf.

"If you are leaving in the umiak," said Inukpuk's wife to

Shulu, "the women here wish to make you a long-tailed sealskin *amoutik* so you can carry that dear child of yours on your back, not in that strange basket."

"*Ahaluna,*" everyone agreed.

"And your husband needs new clothes. Those thin skins he is wearing would never keep him warm at sea. Kungo and the dwarf," she said, "their clothes are worn. You dare not go traveling without new sealskin boots, pants and parkas."

None of the women slept that night, but by midday they had finished cutting and sewing Shulu's beautiful long-tailed parka with its big hood and warm carrying pouch for her child. For Natawa, Kungo and Telikjuak, they had made sleek new sealskin parkas, with pants, mitts and knee-high boots. The red-cheeked girl who was Inukpuk's daughter made a fawn-skin hat for Shulu's baby. That was all the clothing he needed since he would now ride naked against his mother's warm bare back.

The next morning was bright and still with the whole sky clear and blue, from the mountains behind them to the farthest edges of the sea. Long broken lines of drifting ice were turning pink in the low rays of the early morning sun. The sea hunters were busy loading the skin-covered umiak on the river's edge, filling it with gifts of seal and caribou meat and leather bags of birds' eggs packed in eiderdown. When everything was ready, Kungo placed the falcon bow between two of their tight-rolled sleeping skins. Natawa helped put in all the hunting and fishing gear and last of all his paddle and the heavy driftwood oars. They were ready to go.

"You will need a kayak," Inukpuk said to Kungo. "Take this one of mine."

The sea hunters waded out to their boot tops and held the

umiak steady. Natawa helped Shulu climb in with her baby safely riding on her back. Telikjuak gave the umiak a mighty heave, then leaped into its stern and poled out toward the open sea.

Kungo in the kayak paddled after them and the red-cheeked daughter of Inukpuk called out to him, "I hope you come back soon!"

Shulu laughed with excitement as she and Natawa and the powerful dwarf bound the strong oars into their lashings. The box-shaped umiak moved clumsily at first. Shulu smiled when she looked back and saw the red-cheeked girl walking along the water's edge waving good-bye to Kungo.

When they were on the sea, the wind strengthened and Telikjuak pulled the square skin sail up the short mast. They reached the last of the offshore islands and landed just at evening. They cracked open and ate dozens of fresh eggs before they rolled the skin boat over to make a shelter. Lying together in their warm caribou robes, they listened to the sea birds calling through the never-darkening summer twilight.

"This is a good way to live," said Natawa. "I like traveling with you on the sea."

When they woke, the wind was beating like a drummer against the bottom of the umiak and all the birds were gone. Cold scudding clouds swirled just above the water. Kungo put out ahead of them in the kayak, while Natawa helped Telikjuak rig their square sail. Heavy gusts of wind made the umiak run with the waves.

Not until evening did the sea mists blow away and for the first time they could see the island of Tugjak in the distant haze. Shaped like a giant walrus, it hung on the horizon. They pulled the umiak onto a huge flat-topped pan of floating ice. Kungo hauled up the kayak and the men ate seal meat while Shulu fed her child. They walked around on the ice to stretch their cramped legs before they upturned the umiak. They slept through the brief hours of night, then made an early start toward the island.

Above them the sky was changing. Kungo and the dwarf watched anxiously as the wind shifted into the east, then died, leaving an icy calm over the sea. The umiak's sail hung slack.

"I believe a summer storm is coming," Kungo called to the others. "We must try to reach the island first."

"It is still far away," the dwarf exclaimed as he watched stone-gray clouds come rolling toward them. Telikjuak almost broke his oar as he, with the others, tried to make the umiak move faster.

They still had hopes of reaching the safety of the island when Kungo saw the first hard gust of wind come whipping against them, ruffling up the water's surface like a school of leaping silver fish. The second icy blast struck the umiak with such force that the sail split and they almost overturned. Kungo saw Natawa crouched in the bow of the skin boat, his red-bladed paddle flashing, trying to right the umiak. But it was Telikjuak's great strength that turned the umiak away from the island and sent it running with the storm toward the rolling fields of sea ice. The dwarf knew, as did Kungo, that the umiak could never land at Tugjak in the violence of this storm.

They hauled down the torn sail and were driven crookedly with the full force of the storm raging after them. As the umiak lumbered past him, Kungo glanced at Shulu and the others. Even the baby peeking out of the hood looked terrified. Kungo could only try to follow them. He lashed his hunting gear firmly to the kayak deck and puffed more air into his sealskin hunting float. Then slipping out of his knee-high sealskin boots, he blew each boot full of air and bound them tight at the tops with their own drawstrings so that they, too, would act as floats, one on each side of his narrow kayak. Last of all, Kungo lifted up the hem of his sealskin parka and drew it snugly over the small opening of the kayak that fitted around his waist.

Kungo rolled his body and used his long paddle to steady himself as he tried to follow the umiak through the pounding seas. He felt the harsh sting of salt water as it lashed across his face. A second icy wave washed over the deck of the kayak, ripping

loose his bird spear. The wind moaned and screamed around him. Then the whole sea heaved upward as a giant wave struck him in the back, filling his mind with the awful fear of drowning. Kungo looked down at the thin sealskin stretched over the slim driftwood frame of the kayak and thought in horror of the cruel icy deep that lay beneath him. He had lost sight of the umiak mast.

Kungo stopped paddling and put his head down. Using his arm to protect his face, he tried to shut out the terrifying thoughts and sights and sounds that crowded around him. Hearing a tiny squeak, Kungo looked up and saw a small sea pigeon swimming near him. Black and white, it was, with bright red feet and merry yellow eyes. It seemed to be playing, laughing, as it paddled fearlessly on the raging sea. That sight brought Kungo's courage surging back to him.

I can do that, too, thought Kungo, as he paddled strongly with the wind. He shouted with joy when he saw the umiak still afloat. He followed its wildly swaying mast until together they reached the safety of an enormous pan of drifting ice.

Natawa and Shulu were already out, helping Telikjuak pull the umiak to safety. The dwarf then hobbled over and, kneeling, helped Kungo climb out of his kayak.

"It feels good to stand on something solid," Kungo gasped.

"Thank you for bringing all of us here safely," Telikjuak shouted to Seela, the spirit woman who controls the wind. He pointed toward the island which once more seemed far away. "We'll never leave this ice until the storm has passed."

With the wind still rising, the dwarf took the ice chisel and cut two thumb-sized holes in the ice. Then placing the strong harpoon line down in one hole, he pulled it up out of the other, strongly anchoring the umiak so it would not blow away.

"What if this ice breaks?" asked Natawa. Kungo did not answer him.

That night the wind died, but in the morning giant waves still rolled around the ice and dashed against the distant island's cliffs. Natawa had Shulu tell the others that he no longer liked the sea. "Quiet lakes and flowing rivers"—he sighed—"that's water enough for me."

Next day, the clouds had rolled away and the sea round them lay still as ice. The night tides had carried the ice much closer to the island. Towing the kayak behind them, they all four rowed the umiak toward the island. So overjoyed was Pudlat when he saw them, that he came leaping down the rough stone path, surrounded by Kungo's team of white wolf dogs. When they landed, he helped Shulu with her baby out of the umiak. The others followed and they all helped to draw the boats to safety, weighting them down with stones against new winds that might come and blow them out to sea. The wolf dogs around Kungo were sniffing and bending excitedly. He called them all by name.

Each carrying as much as possible, the others followed Kungo up the rising island path. The old man, Ittok, and his wife stood waiting outside the entrance to their whalebone house. Kungo ran to greet them.

"*Tikiposi*, you arrive!" Luvi Luvi La exclaimed.

Ittok reached out with his hands and touched Kungo. "Is it really you, and Telikjuak as well?" the blind man whispered. "We almost lost all hope of your returning."

"Three different reasons brought me back to you," said Kungo. "First, the pleasure of being near you once again. Second, to show you my sister, Shulu, her child, and this True Man who is her husband, Natawa. And finally, to return the falcon bow."

Kungo pressed the big bow and the quiver of arrows into Ittok's hands.

"All of you, come down into the house," said the old woman. "Your clothes are wet and rimmed with salt."

It was safe and warm inside and Shulu eased her infant from her back and fed him. "His name is Kungo," she said proudly.

The old woman laughed and rubbed noses with the new child, and sang it an ancient song:

> Ayii, Ayii, Ayii, Ayii,
> When the raven
> Became aware of himself,
> Light came into the world
> And the tufts of grass
> Turned into men.
> Ayii, Ayii.

The baby laughed, then looked wise as though it had understood each word.

When they had eaten all the food that they desired and slept, Kungo and the dwarf told them all that had happened in the caribou country and how lightning, not the Indians, had caused the fires, and how the caribou had returned to the seacoast, and the fish were running up the river once again.

When their story was over, the old man lay back like some ancient spirit of the sea with his white hair spread across his shoulders. "That is as it should be," he said, smiling toward his guests.

His wife, Sandpiper, sat quietly by her lamp, braiding a new bowstring.

Next morning, Telikjuak and Pudlat each took small lighted

seal-oil lamps and showed Natawa and Shulu some of the dark caves and passages that curved back endlessly into the island's rock.

"Tell your husband," Pudlat said, "that this island is a magic place. Some nights I felt like howling with these wolf dogs at the moon man's face. There is no need for me to stay longer. I will take the kayak and return to my family at Inukpuk's camp."

Later, inside the whalebone house, the old man gently stroked the winglike curves of the mighty falcon bow.

"That bow could never be mine," said Kungo. "It has a mind of its own."

The old man turned his head and held the bow against his ear, nodding in time as though he heard it singing. "White Archer, I believe your troubled childhood lies behind you. Perhaps you do not need this bow, even though it has a new string. Here, take the falcon bow outside."

Above Kungo's head a faint drift of evening clouds were reflected in the cold blue stillness of the sea around them.

The old man held up his hand to silence the others, then cocked his head. "White Archer, do you see a raven?"

Kungo looked carefully around him. "I see nothing."

"Listen carefully. Do you not hear him ruffling his feathers? He must be sitting over there."

Natawa, whose eyes were eagle sharp, peered into the shadows by the furthest cave. "Yes, I see him now," he whispered, and pointed to the raven.

At that moment, the raven gave a rough "carrouk."

"Launch an arrow at him," cried the old man.

"I do not wish to kill a raven," Kungo answered.

"That raven is very old," said Ittok. "He knows how to protect himself from men."

The dwarf drew an arrow from the quiver and notched it to the bowstring. The White Archer closed his eyes and waited for the power to come to him, then raised the great horn bow and drew it to its fullest curve. Twang! went the bow. The watchers leaped back in surprise. The falcon bow, like the arrow, burst into a flash of light. Out of the smoke and flames, Shulu and all the others saw the sharp beak and eye, the speckled breast and the swept-back wings of a true white falcon as it flew out of Kungo's hands. Gathering speed, it hurtled past the gray stone cliffs, diving straight toward the raven. The wily raven leaped from its perch and flew toward the mainland, cunningly twisting and turning to escape the plunging swiftness of the falcon.

Kungo gasped as he held out his empty hands to the old man.

Ittok exclaimed, "The falcon is free to fly once more."

"Will it catch that raven?" Kungo asked him.

"I do not know," said the old man, "but I am glad that they both fly free."

The old woman took her husband gently by the arm and helped him toward their house.

Inside, Kungo and Shulu pleaded with them to return to the mainland. "You cannot stay here alone," said Shulu. "Come and let us care for you."

"This island is our home," said Luvi Luvi La.

Ittok reached out and touched his wife's hand, then said, "Yes, perhaps we should leave with you when Pudlat goes."

"That could be tomorrow," Kungo told them. "This light west wind would carry us swiftly to the mainland."

Shulu whispered to her baby, "Good! We will go together. That umiak has space enough for us and Kungo's dogs as well."

Luvi Luvi La smiled at Shulu and said to her baby, "Be a

good man like your father, and take good care of your mother."
Shulu wondered at her words as she lay down on the wide bed
and went to sleep.

The house was cold when Kungo's sister woke him. "Where
are they?" she asked him. "Where has the old man gone? Where's
his wife?"

"They must be outside," said Kungo, "getting ready for the
voyage."

"They have taken nothing from this house," said Shulu, pointing at their neatly folded clothing. "Why would she have let her
lamp go out?"

Kungo sat up, pulling on his boots, pants and parka, then hurried outside. Shulu followed him. The dwarf and Pudlat were busy coiling sealskin line.

"Have you seen them?" Kungo called.

"No," Pudlat grunted, not looking up at Kungo.

"Where are they?" Shulu cried.

"I do not know," the dwarf answered. "Are you surprised that they are gone?"

Kungo and Shulu ran from one dark cave to another, calling into each. But only the hollow echo of their voices came back to them. Gasping for breath, they ran back to the dwarf. "What could have happened to them?"

"Who can say." The dwarf sighed. "This is not the first time they have disappeared." He spread his arms toward the whalebone house, then grinned at Kungo slyly. "This is their island, their home. Perhaps this is their way of telling you they do not wish to leave."

"You must help us find them," Shulu said.

The dwarf shrugged his shoulders. "How could I? That old man is nearly blind, but he knows these hidden caves far better than any man with sight."

"They cannot stay here all alone," cried Kungo.

"Oh, yes they could," said Telikjuak. "But I will never leave them." He smiled again at Kungo. "I, too, belong here on this island. I will stay and care for them."

The dwarf reached out and taking Kungo beneath the arms, he lifted him high above his head. "You are truly the best friend I have ever had. When you and these others sail away, I shall miss you more than I can say. Go, White Archer. You shall be always inside of me. Return with the others to the sea hunters' camp. Ask Inukpuk if he will some day let you marry his red-cheeked daughter."

"It is time to go," Pudlat shouted as he hurried down the path.

Kungo saw Pudlat ease the umiak into the water then turn and shout to the dwarf, "I leave my kayak as a gift to you."

Kungo looked into the dwarf's face for the last time. He tried to speak, but the words caught in his throat.

"I will never forget the wonderful journeys we have shared together," said Telikjuak. Then he turned away so none of them would see him weeping.

A cold breeze swept in from the sea as Kungo, with his dogs around him, walked to the cove. There Natawa, and Shulu with her child, and Pudlat stood waiting for him. With a word from Kungo, the white wolf dogs leaped into the boat. The others followed.

Kungo stepped out on the farthest kayak stone, gave the umiak a long smooth push, then jumped aboard. Pudlat hauled up a new skin sail and its belly filled with the fair wind.

As they passed the tall headland of Tugjak Island, they looked back and saw sea birds rising in noisy flocks from the steep stone cliffs.

"There he is!" screamed Shulu, pointing up to the top of the rock ridge where the two ancient stone *inukshuks* stood.

Yes, all of them could see the dwarf hobbling up the narrow path toward the pair of gray stone statues. Each person in the skin boat waved at Telikjuak, then froze in open-mouthed astonishment. At the top of the steep stone cliff face, they saw Ittok and his wife step out from behind the two stone statues.

The dwarf spread his arms and let out a mighty roar of triumph. "I have found them," Telikjuak shouted, his voice soaring on the wind. "Farewell, farewell."

The strong sail carried the umiak farther and farther from the island. Those in the boat watched in wonder as the powerful dwarf helped the old man and his wife down the steep path that led toward their home. Kungo and his sister dried their eyes, and, like the others, turned their heads toward the mainland, eagerly searching for the new lives that lay before them.